She waited to see what he would dare do next....

"Do you know what the first rule of the game is, according to Ovid?"

"No." How could he expect her to worry about the wafflings of a centuries-dead Roman poet when she could feel the rise and fall of his chest lightly tantalizing her breasts?

Jack shifted, his hip wedging against her inner thigh as he took his weight on one arm and lifted the other to run his finger over her damp mouth as he told her with a lazy sexual arrogance, "Women can always be caught."

"So can men."

"So we can. So I suppose it boils down to who is more eager to do the catching in each individual case. Who is being caught here, Beth? You or me?"

THE
HAWK

SUSAN NAPIER was born on St. Valentine's Day, so it's not surprising that she's developed an enduring love of romantic stories. She started her writing career as a journalist in Auckland, New Zealand, trying her hand at romance fiction only after she had married her handsome boss! Numerous books later she still lives with her most enduring hero, two future heroes—her sons!—two cats and a computer. When she's not writing, she likes to read and cook, often simultaneously!

Books by Susan Napier

HARLEQUIN PRESENTS
1380—NO REPRIEVE
1460—DEAL OF A LIFETIME
1483—DEVIL TO PAY
1531—TEMPT ME NOT
1554—SECRET ADMIRER
1595—WINTER OF DREAMS

HARLEQUIN ROMANCE
2711—LOVE IN THE VALLEY
2723—SWEET VIXEN

Susan Napier

THE HAWK AND THE LAMB

Harlequin Books

TORONTO • NEW YORK • LONDON
AMSTERDAM • PARIS • SYDNEY • HAMBURG
STOCKHOLM • ATHENS • TOKYO • MILAN
MADRID • WARSAW • BUDAPEST • AUCKLAND

ISBN 0-373-11616-0

THE HAWK AND THE LAMB

Copyright © 1993 by Susan Napier.

Printed in U.S.A.

CHAPTER ONE

BY THE time the jet had climbed to thirty-five thousand feet Elizabeth Lamb had resigned herself to the destruction of her secret fantasies. She would make a terrible spy. A life of glamorous intrigue and spine-tingling excitement was definitely not for her. Why, the plane hadn't even levelled off yet and she was desperate for the drinks trolley to come around so that she might steady her shattered nerves with a savage slug of pure, potent alcohol.

Elizabeth forced her hands to relax in her lap and allowed her clever brain to attack the problem from another angle. She wasn't incompetent—or insane. She was doing what had to be done. She had never dealt well with surprises and the one that had been sprung on her at the airport had been bound temporarily to unnerve her. In the circumstances she was handling herself rather well.

She grimaced. Perhaps that was a *slight* exaggeration. She had been trying to behave with the utmost discretion, to attract as little attention as possible to herself—a task that she usually accomplished effortlessly—and had bungled it badly. First there had been the altercation at the check-in desk when the harassed airline representative had tried to tell her that because she was a few minutes late checking in there was no longer a seat available for her. If she were travelling purely on her own behalf Elizabeth would have happily accepted the offer of a later flight, but as it was she had had no choice but to make a fuss until the airline had backed down. Unfortunately the fuss had generated a ripple of interest through the surrounding queues of semi-bored travellers including the small, disdainful queue of first-class passengers at the adjacent desk.

Then there had been the incident at the security checkpoint in the departure hall. Elizabeth had set the alarms screaming as she walked through the scanning arch. She had been made to walk through twice more, each time becoming more flustered, before the security officer had run his hand-scanner over her and asked politely if she was wearing any jewellery under her clothes.

Elizabeth had clapped a hand to her chest, her whole body going hot with guilt. 'Yes, but it's gold—a necklace—surely it wouldn't set *that* thing off,' she said in her distinctively deep voice.

'It may have some other metal mixed in with it; may I see?' the officer asked in a bored tone that didn't reassure Elizabeth's anxieties at all. He obviously didn't think she was a criminal type, but his opinion might change when he saw what she was wearing!

She unbuttoned the neck of her blouse cautiously, conscious of the curious eyes around them, some sympathetic, most amused and one casual silver-grey glance she was most particularly anxious to avoid. She turned protectively away from the passing crowd as she opened the blouse to show the guard what she was wearing, feeling embarrassingly like a flasher as he looked into her parted clothing. His eyes flicked up to her flushed face and down again.

'Looks rather valuable.'

'It is,' Elizabeth admitted in an agony of apprehension. 'It's—sort of a family heirloom. That's why I'm wearing it. I didn't like to put it in my luggage.'

To her eternal gratitude he didn't ask *whose* family heirloom. The officer ran his scanner over her chest and it beeped obligingly. The metal it was detecting was probably the hard, cold lump of terror in her chest where her warm, pulsing heart used to be! 'You're probably wise, ma'am. Going on holiday or business?'

'Oh, holiday,' she said only semi-truthfully. 'To Nouméa—the Isle of Hawks, actually.' Her name-dropping would explain the necklace if the man knew anything about New Caledonia. The off-shore resort was renowned for the glamour of its nightclub and casino.

He turned and had a murmured word with his senior colleague who moved obligingly over and peered into Elizabeth's exposed cleavage, making her acutely aware of the fullness of her breasts. This man wasn't in the least bored and the faint gleam in his eye told Elizabeth he knew exactly what was going through her mind to make her blush. Or thought he did. If he had known *everything* he would have arrested her on the spot!

'Would you mind taking off your sunglasses for a moment, ma'am?' the second man asked, and Elizabeth did so, reluctantly, hurriedly re-buttoning her blouse as one of the more curious spectators edged around to see what the men were finding so interesting.

The officer cleared his throat, staring into her guilty eyes.

Oh, God, he could read her like a book. He was trained to detect the give-away signs of incipient panic. He was going to make his move now. Drag her away in front of all these people for an interrogation and full body-search.

Instead he smiled at her, the gleam now full-blown admiration. 'Did anyone ever tell you that you have Elizabeth Taylor eyes?'

'I—er—yes, no—that's my name—Elizabeth, I mean,' she fumbled, aghast at this sudden personal interest. She knew her big violet eyes with their thick, dark brows were her most memorable feature—that was why she was trying to hide them.

Luckily some other innocent traveller triggered the security alarm and Elizabeth took advantage of the moment to walk away with her fragile calm still intact. Her spine prickled all the way from skull to coccyx as she did so, expecting any moment to feel the heavy hand of the law on her shoulder. It took all her concentration not to break into a frenzied dash as she approached the foreign exchange window and exchanged her few remaining New Zealand dollars for the Pacific French francs used in New Caledonia.

She then scuttled into the crowded departure lounge, sure that she was over the worst, only to stumble over a stray suitcase and knock a young child's paper cup of water flying. The little boy burst into tears and Elizabeth cringed as everyone stared at her, assessing her culpability as a bully. Her furtive effort to bribe the child back into smiles with the offer of a tiny, crumpled pack of sweets earned her a suspicious look and a tart refusal from his parent. Feeling like a convicted child-molester, she slunk into the nearest available seat and discovered the man with the silver-grey eyes sitting directly across from her, idly watching her flustered arrival.

Hastily she raised the magazine she had bought to read on the plane in front of her flushed face and took several deep breaths under the contemptuous gaze of a rail-thin model who looked as if she didn't know what a blush was. Elizabeth had never wanted to be a model herself, but that wasn't to say she wouldn't have liked the option of being a great beauty. However, a lovely pair of eyes didn't offset a regrettable lack of vertical inches and a superfluity of horizontal ones. Not that she felt physically insignificant. Quite the reverse. Up until she was thirteen she had always been the tallest girl in class and by the time her friends' growth spurts had overtaken her own it was too late, her mindset was fixed. She had always thought of herself as tall, and tall was the way she acted—with a little help from the footwear industry. She was the tallest five-foot-six woman she knew.

The seatbelt sign pinged off now as the jet achieved its cruising height for the three-hour flight and Elizabeth unrolled her tortured magazine and opened it to take her mind off the laggardly drinks trolley. The self-same haughty model, now stretched invitingly out on some namelessly beautiful Caribbean beach, sneered up at her, and she sneered back. Soon Elizabeth, too, would be lolling without a care in the world on warm white sands lapped by a crystal lagoon, the wettest New Zealand winter on record a mere memory...providing she could take care of one or two little matters first! She might not have a gorgeous, tanned, muscle-bound and no doubt muscle-brained beach-boy to loll about with like the model, but she had something much more satisfying, not to mention healthy—a pile of bestsellers that she had been dying to read for months.

Of course, if Marge had accompanied her on this holiday as had been planned, Elizabeth might have ended up with both, but part of her was secretly relieved that she could now be thoroughly selfish and unsociable if she chose. Marge found it difficult to believe that any woman could be satisfied without a man in her life, but Elizabeth knew better than to believe that there was a designated 'Mr Right' for every woman. There had always been a surfeit of men in her life. She didn't regard them, as Marge did, as excitingly mysterious or challengingly elusive. She understood them all too well and found them comfortingly but sometimes tiresomely predictable. She enjoyed their company but never made the mistake of taking them seriously. Elizabeth's job as a researcher and assistant to a professor of literature at Auckland University meant that she was surrounded by intelligent young men and women, many of whom took themselves far too seriously and paid the price for it in unnecessary suffering, both physical and mental. But then anguish was supposed to be good for the soul. If so Elizabeth's soul was obviously as indolent as the rest of her.

'Double gin and tonic, please.' Elizabeth roused herself to give her order to the air hostess who had bent enquiringly over her seat.

'Miss Lamb?' Belatedly Elizabeth noticed the lack of a trolley. Instead the woman held a piece of paper headed with the airline's logo, her French accent somehow making her words sound more ominous. 'I wonder if you would mind coming forward with me?'

Elizabeth froze. 'Er——'

'And could you bring your things? Do you have any hand luggage in the overhead carrier?'

Elizabeth shook her head blankly, indicating the handbag and camera case down by her feet, her heart racing all over again. 'Is something wrong? Am I in the wrong seat?'

'In a manner of speaking,' the hostess murmured blandly, with a soothing smile at the surrounding passengers. 'If you'll just follow me—don't forget your jacket!'

Elizabeth turned and picked up the light, knitted-cotton jacket that she had shed on her seat, clutching her shoulder-bag and camera tightly to her chest as she followed the hostess up the aisle, conscious that she had somehow managed, yet again, to draw attention to herself. Was she being taken to see the pilot? Perhaps she was going to be handed a parachute and tossed off the plane! Or perhaps she was going to be clapped in irons for the duration of the flight.

'I didn't want to say anything in front of the other passengers,' murmured the hostess as she paused by the small galley ahead of the compact business-class section, and Elizabeth's nerves shivered. 'Some people get

very annoyed if there's any hint of inequity but...
you've been upgraded to first class!'

With something of a dramatic flourish she drew back
the curtain which divided ⁺he privileged from the ple-
beian and indicated the rear aisle seat. 'If you'd like to
sit down I'll bring you a glass of champagne and the
lunch menu.'

'But... I'm sure there must be some mistake,' quavered Elizabeth, aghast at this new development.

'No mistake.' The hostess looked surprised, as well
she might. No one in her right mind would turn down
the offer of a first-class ride at economy-class rates.
Heads were already turning. Elizabeth realised that if
she continued to protest she was going to make herself
even more conspicuous than she had already. The
woman glanced at the note in her hand. 'I believe you
must have a friend in our public relations division,' she
offered smilingly. 'That's where the suggestion came
from to upgrade you if we had any available spare
seats.'

Duncan Frazer! Elizabeth was hard put to it not to
scream her frustration. Uncle Miles must have told his
friend about her travel plans... his way of making up
for the unfortunate position he had placed her in. Little
did he know the even more unfortunate position he had
placed her in now.

For, as Elizabeth reluctantly moved to take her place
in unwonted luxury, there—sitting in the window seat
studying his newly acquired travelling companion with
speculative deliberation—was the very man whom she
had been at such extreme pains to detect and avoid.

The man whom she was supposed to be surreptitiously following, spying on and secretly photographing.

The man she was supposed to expose as a lying, cheating adulterer.

Jean-Jules Hawkwood.

The man with pure silver eyes and a heart as black as sin.

CHAPTER TWO

HANDSOME as sin, too. That was a shock. It hadn't been Elizabeth's first impression on seeing him at the airport, or even her second. He wasn't particularly tall for a man, probably around five feet ten, and in the coat he had been wearing he had looked rather bulky. The pony-tail and the earring had been the crowning factors in her dismissal of him as vain and effete. But now he was stripped to jeans and a contoured pale blue shirt she could see that his bulk was all muscle and his hairstyle only served to emphasise the uncompromisingly harsh maleness of his body and face. The sleek blue-black hair drawn ruthlessly back into the small pony-tail at the nape of his neck revealed a face of almost sculpted starkness, all slashing bone and tautly stretched skin. His mouth was wide but his lips were narrow, their thinness adding to the impression of harshness, even cruelty. The earring was a thin gold circle in his right ear. If she hadn't known that he was a wealthy businessman Elizabeth would have pegged him as a man who lived outside the law—lean and mean and definitely dangerous to know. Someone totally outside her limited experience. A pony-tail, for goodness' sake! Admittedly it was only a couple of inches long, which meant that his hair would barely cover his collar, but still, it was so...*menacing*! It made him look like a drug-dealer or gun-runner, the kind of man who enjoyed living on a perpetual knife-edge of legality... of risk.

'Miss Lamb?'

The dark-eyed air hostess was frowning in puzzlement as Elizabeth's hesitation stretched several seconds too long.

'Er—yes, thank you very much.' Her normally deep voice was even huskier than usual, prompting a flicker of curiosity in that lightning-silver gaze. Elizabeth sat down hastily, ignoring him with rigid deliberation as she fumbled blindly at her left hip for the seatbelt clip, unwilling to turn her head even a fraction of an inch to the side even when she began to doubt that her seat *possessed* a safety-belt. It was a shock when a warm, masculine hand suddenly tangled her searching fingers.

She gasped, jerking her hand back, resisting the natural compulsion to look at him, looking down instead at the blunt, scarred fingers which proffered the elusive device, her smooth, shoulder-length brown hair sliding forward to hide the flush in her cheeks.

'Thank you,' she muttered gracelessly, grabbing at it, careful not to touch him again.

'You're welcome.' His English was impeccable, as was the subtle sardonic emphasis that mocked her apparent rudeness.

Elizabeth fastened her seatbelt and sat, stiff-backed, her handbag and camera clutched in her lap. Out of the corner of her eye she could see that her quarry already had his glass of champagne. He lifted it out of range of her peripheral eyesight and she thought hopefully that maybe he was a lush and would drink enough on the voyage to forget having sat beside her. She also noted that there was no wedding band on his ring-finger. Typical. As a rich man he probably decked his wife in symbols of his possession but he didn't want to advertise his own marital status—it would cramp his style!

Feeling uncomfortable with her thoughts, Elizabeth bent to put her handbag and camera case underneath her feet, inadvertently tangling the strap of the camera on the delicate heel of her shoe and somehow looping it around her ankle. Her narrow skirt made it difficult to shake the impediment loose even after she shed her shoe, and she had to struggle to free herself mostly by touch since the dark glasses rendered the dimness below seat level almost totally black. When she finally achieved success she bobbed up again with relief, her shoulder knocking the glass of champagne that the hostess was patiently waiting to serve her out of her hand. The glass up-ended on to Elizabeth's breasts, the sparkling liquid instantly moulding her cream blouse semi-transparently against her skin.

'Oh, Miss Lamb, I'm awfully sorry,' the hostess cried in genuine dismay.

If Elizabeth had paid for first-class she might not have been so gracious, but in the circumstances she was anxious to smooth things over as quickly as possible.

'That's all right, it was completely my fault; please— don't worry about it . . .'

She dabbed feebly at the wet fabric with the cocktail napkin which the hostess had handed her before quickly hurrying away to fetch something more substantial, cursing the love of extravagant underwear that had prompted her to wear a particularly daring lace bra in 'mood indigo' under the demure blouse. The only saving grace was that the material across her collarbone had only been slightly splashed, thereby still concealing the precious cargo encircling her neck.

A white handkerchief, exquisitely pressed and embroidered with the initials 'J.H.', appeared under her nose.

'Oh, no, it's all right, I can manage.' Elizabeth turned her head away from the offer, unwilling to be beholden, even in such a trifle, to one such as he.

'I assure you it is clean. Quite uncontaminated,' came the crisp rejoinder. His English was slightly less impeccable this time, barely containing his irritation.

'I wouldn't want to dirty it——'

'Champagne is hardly likely to do that. Quite the reverse—some people even bath in the stuff, you know...'

Elizabeth suddenly had a startling vision of that lean, hard, amoral body lounging in a bath of the foaming, golden fluid...not alone, of course...

Appalled at her wayward imagination, she held on to her dogged resistance. 'I don't think——'

'Obviously not. All the while you are arguing so pointlessly with me your garments are becoming saturated beyond saving. I would have thought that modesty alone would have overcome your scruples about my laundry.'

Elizabeth's head jerked up and she looked squarely at him for the first time. The silver-grey eyes seemed to penetrate her protective dark mask for a fraction of a second before they lowered mockingly to her breasts. Her hands rose automatically to shield herself but before she could place them across her chest her tormentor had shaken out the neat folds of his handkerchief and draped it gracefully across the provocative indigo pattern traced by the transparent fabric. She clutched it to her soaked body as he murmured, 'Have you something else to change into? I'm sure the air hostess will find some way to dry your blouse for you by the time we reach Nouméa.'

'I—no,' said Elizabeth grudgingly, thinking of her buttonless jacket.

At that moment the hostess returned with a small towel and Elizabeth held it gratefully against her rapidly cooling chest, blotting up the worst of the moisture while extricating the now sodden handkerchief. Should she offer to have it dry-cleaned?

The decision was taken out of her hands when the air hostess spoke across the top of her head in French, graciously offering to have the handkerchief drycleaned with Elizabeth's blouse, calling the man 'Monsieur Hawkwood' with a familiarity that implied he was a frequent flyer with Air Caledonie. The man responded with a lazily flirtatious remark and in the course of their exchange reiterated his suggestion that Elizabeth change out of her wet blouse.

Elizabeth opened her mouth to tell him that she was perfectly capable of making her own request when he cut her off with a condescending smile and a rough translation, minus the flirtatious bits, of the conversation. He obviously assumed that Elizabeth was a naïve scatter-brain who couldn't possibly have mastered another language, and she closed her mouth again when she realised that his erroneous assumption could be to her advantage. If he didn't know that she spoke his language fluently he might inadvertently betray something useful in her hearing.

At the hostess's urging Elizabeth slipped into the compact toilet to remove her blouse and rinse both it and her slightly sticky breasts. She took off the necklace and very carefully washed it, marvelling anew at the fine workmanship that had gone into the ornately wrought settings and triangular gold links of the supporting chain. The diamonds and blood-red rubies glittered brilliantly in her hands but Elizabeth felt only unease at the recognition of their beauty. Why, the stones alone were probably worth tens of thousands of dollars!

Her bra was also damp but she had no intention of removing that, too. For one thing her full breasts always felt uncomfortable without firm support. For another, J.J. Hawkwood made her feel self-conscious enough without the added awkwardness of feeling physically vulnerable.

Therefore she was appalled when the air hostess passed her the promised replacement shirt through a crack in the door—*not* one from a spare crew uniform as Elizabeth had expected but 'kindly lent by Monsieur Hawkwood, who always carries a full change of clothes'. Elizabeth longed to reject the offer but had already handed over her blouse. The shirt wasn't of an inexpensive polyester variety either—it was pure silk, white, softly draping from narrow gathers on the yoked shoulders. The label proclaimed it custom-made. The sleeves hung well down over her hands but Elizabeth had to roll them up anyway because the cuffs only had slits for cuff-links, no buttons.

Elizabeth smoothed her dark brown hair unnecessarily, putting off the moment when she would have to step out of the door. Her lipstick had worn off and the lower part of her face under her thick fringe and concealing sunglasses looked far too pale. She took the sunglasses off. That was even worse. Her eyes looked huge and bruised in her pale face, a little wild and definitely fearful. A dead give-away in fact. She bit her lips to try and give them a bit of colour but they only seemed to emphasise what she had always felt was a too-small mouth. Everything about her looked somehow out of kilter, which was exactly how she felt.

She buttoned the shirt right up to the small stand-up collar but still it looked far too... sexy. The shirt was too big, of course, but instead of concealing her curves the thin shroud of silk seemed to settle lovingly against them every time she moved. Even in these days of unisex dressing there was something *risqué* about wearing a man's shirt, Elizabeth thought glumly. Something challenging, and the last thing she wanted was for J.J. Hawkwood to think she was challenging him in any way whatsoever.

Elizabeth sighed. If only Marge hadn't fallen ill she wouldn't be in this mess.

When Uncle Simon had unexpectedly turned up to run her out to the airport earlier that morning she hadn't at first suspected an ulterior motive. She had merely thought that he wanted to save his two elder brothers the rush-hour trip across town. At seventy-two and seventy-five respectively Miles and Seymour Lamb generally preferred someone else to drive them around in their lovingly cared for vintage Citroën— usually Elizabeth herself.

Uncle Simon had allowed her to say her farewells to the two old men in blissful ignorance, waiting until they were on their way to the airport to drop his bomb-shell.

'Marge can't go with you.'

'What?' Elizabeth turned her shocked face towards his profile and he gave her the reassuring 'everything'll be all right, Jake' grin that usually meant the opposite.

'If you've suddenly found some urgent work for her I hope she quits and comes anyway,' Elizabeth said furiously. 'She hasn't had a holiday for sixteen months ' Marge Benson was Simon's secretary-receptionist and general dogsbody, and Elizabeth often felt that her uncle didn't truly appreciate the extent of her friend's dedication and loyalty.

'No—nothing like that,' her uncle told her hurriedly. 'She woke up this morning with some horrendous variety of flu. She got her doctor to make a house-call and he refused to give her clearance to fly for at least a week. She knew that you'd be upset so instead of ringing she asked me to tell you . . .'

'But why didn't you let me know earlier?' Elizabeth cried in dismay. 'If we try and cancel now I'll probably have to forfeit most of my fare!' That was no small sum. The resort at which they were booked was highly exclusive and air fare, accommodation, meals and entertainment were all included in the cost.

Her next unpalatable thought was that she *couldn't* cancel, anyway. Too much depended on her going to New Caledonia as soon as possible.

'You can't cancel!' her uncle unknowingly echoed her thoughts. 'I mean, you don't *have* to,' he corrected himself hastily. 'Marge *insists* that you go; she'll feel awfully guilty if you don't. Just because she's sick is no reason that you should have to lose out. You've been looking forward to a holiday for ages and you had to juggle a whole load of schedules to get this leave. You originally intended going by yourself, anyway. And the weather here is awful at the moment—you wouldn't have much of a holiday at home. What with having just got over the flu yourself you *need* to get completely away for a good rest. What better place than a sub-tropical island in the South Pacific?'

Elizabeth was touched by his fervent concern until he added sheepishly, 'And . . . well, *I* need you to go.'

In spite of her questions he refused to be any more forthcoming until they got to the airport, his craggy face taking on the familiar look of pugnacious determination that served him so well in his profession. After racketing around the world in a variety of jobs in his youth and then doing a five-year stint in the army, in middle age Uncle Simon had surprised his family by settling down to run a detective agency in Auckland.

At the terminal, Elizabeth balked at checking in, steering her uncle instead to the coffee shop and insisting he explain himself, which he did, at exhaustive length.

Marge, it seemed, had jumped at the offer to accompany Elizabeth to the Isle of Hawks in New Caledonia not just because she wanted a holiday, but because it was timely cover for the budding detective to carry out a small 'job' for her boss. She was supposed to bring back photographic evidence of an errant wife's affair with *her* married boss—who happened to be none other than Jean-Jules Hawkwood, head of the corporation which owned the international chain of exclusive Hawk Hotels.

Elizabeth was appalled. 'What do you mean, photographic *evidence*?' She had visions of Marge hiding in closets and jumping out on the lovers.

'Just shots of them together that might show they're more than just colleagues,' her uncle said soothingly. 'My client has suspected his wife of being unfaithful for a while but he doesn't want to confront her until he's sure that he's right. He's not looking for divorce evidence; in fact he hopes he can *save* his marriage by confronting her with the truth. His wife is pretty high up in local management for Hawk Hotels, so trips to the flagship resort at Ile de Faucons for seminars and meetings are not unusual. But my client accidentally discovered that, contrary to what she told him, there isn't any seminar this time—that the ten days she's spending up there is being salaried as "holiday pay" and that Hawkwood is going with her. She hadn't mentioned *that* little titbit either...'

'What about Hawkwood's wife? Where is she?'

'In France. She lives on her family's estate there most of the year, along with their three school-age children, while Hawkwood spends most of his time living out of Hawk Hotels all over the world. Actually the corporation is registered in New Caledonia—Nouméa is his official residence as far as tax records are concerned—but he only spends sufficient time there to qualify for citizenship. It's all in the file.'

Elizabeth looked at the buff-coloured envelope her uncle slid across the table towards her. 'What are you giving it to me for?'

Her uncle smiled hopefully.

'No, oh, no!' She realised his intention and pushed the envelope back towards him, shaking her head vigorously. 'No, you can't ask me to do this, Uncle Simon——'

He pushed it back. 'Why not? You've done little tasks for me before...'

'Yes, *easy* ones—research jobs, gathering information from files—organisational things that I know I'm *good* at——'

'But wouldn't you like to try your hand at some real detection? You love spy novels and TV detective shows. Now's your chance to try it for yourself. Who knows? You might find yourself with a new career!'

'I'm well aware of the difference between fantasy and reality, Uncle Simon,' Elizabeth said firmly. 'I may enjoy reading about murder and mayhem but that doesn't mean I want to strap on a gun and risk life and limb to battle real-life baddies. I like my thrills to be strictly vicarious!'

At twenty-five, Elizabeth thought of herself as more mature than most women her age, less physically adventurous and more...*settled*. While she had indeed sometimes envied Marge the unpredictability of her job, the minor upheavals of excitement and intrigue that spiced her life, on the whole Elizabeth was quite satisfied with her own comparatively mundane lot.

She had been brought up in a very old-fashioned and yet also very unusual fashion by two middle-aged uncles whose consuming interests in life were intellectual. Seymour and Miles Lamb loved books with a passion, and had instinctively passed that love on to the child unexpectedly placed in their charge after her parents' death when she was four. Thus from a young age Elizabeth had been taught to revere learning. She had found that for every question there was an answer to be found in the pages of the books which were crammed, floor to ceiling, in her uncles' second-hand bookshop—rare first editions cheek by jowl with dog-eared paperbacks and musty tomes by some long-forgotten author whose only claim to interest lay in the lavish leather bindings of his turgid prose. She hadn't felt the restless need to travel as had many of her generation in their late teens, because she had already travelled the world in her mind without leaving the comfort and security of the cluttered shop or the roomy old book-crammed apartment upstairs where the three of them lived.

Besides, Seymour and Miles had needed her. They were capable, intelligent men, but they were slaves to their passion. In good times it had been enough for them to run Lamb's Tales more as a hobby than as a proper business, but when the recession had hit it had taken Elizabeth's practical common sense to sort out that their problems were largely caused by the two men acquiring rare books that they were then loath to part with, jealously guarding them against potential customers. Elizabeth had even known Seymour to patrol the shelves and snatch a book out of browser's hand if he considered that the person wasn't truly appreciative of what he held. Only certain hand-picked customers were worthy of being offered the best, and profits had suffered accordingly.

As her uncles grew older and even more eccentric in their habits, Elizabeth had gradually taken on more and more of the workload, sandwiching it between her flexible hours at the university, until she was virtually managing the store and doing all the bothersome paperwork that her uncles had too frequently neglected and leaving them free to go on the buying expeditions that they so richly enjoyed. Elizabeth was enormously proud of the reputation that Lamb's Tales was building in the rare and second-hand book trade. When she finally inherited the bookstore she intended to make it her full-time career.

'Oh, come on, girl, it's not as if I'm asking you to do anything dangerous or illegal; the only thing you'll be armed with is a perfectly harmless camera,' Uncle Simon coaxed, producing a fearsomely professional-looking camera-case and placing it on top of the envelope between them.

'It's not complicated—all you have to do is point it and click; the camera does the rest. Truly, Beth, you'd be doing me a tremendous favour, and Marge of course—she feels *awfully* guilty about letting me down...

'I've met Hawkwood personally otherwise *I'd* have done the job in the first place, but I can't risk him recognising me and there's no one else I can send on such short notice even if I *could* switch the bookings. Naturally I'll reimburse you for your fare and expenses. All I want is a few casual shots of the two of them on holiday!'

'*Compromising* shots,' Elizabeth clarified tartly, sorely tempted by the thought that she might be able to afford a totally stress-and-obligation-free holiday later in the year if she accepted his offer. At the rate this trip was deteriorating she might need one as soon as she returned!

'Not necessarily. I'm paid to find out the truth, not manufacture evidence. I can't believe that you'd think I would ask you to do that,' her uncle replied with an air of offended dignity that didn't fool her for a moment. If Uncle Simon thought he could shame her into helping him he would play the injured innocent to the hilt.

On the other hand she had already agreed to help Uncle Miles out of a far more unpleasant situation. How could she justify turning her back on Uncle Simon in *his* hour of need? He hadn't had as much of a hand in her raising as his brothers but on his travels he had sent her letters and postcards and exotic presents from every far-flung corner of the globe.

She sighed. 'I'm not trained to be sneaky like you and Marge——'

'I know; all I'm asking you to do is keep an eye on their activities. If they're intimate it's bound to affect the way they behave in public. They probably won't feel the need to be too careful on Hawkwood's home territory—his father was English but his mother is French New Caledonian and it's her family who put up the money for Hawk Hotels—that's why the first and reputedly still the best resort was built there...they even changed the name of the island to celebrate its original opening.' Uncle Simon's voice lowered as he attacked her rapidly weakening resistance head-on.

'Jean-Jules Hawkwood is rich and powerful and can and does probably have anything—and any woman— he wants, whereas my client's wife is his whole *world*. From what I can discover from a couple of Hawkwood's other ex-lovers he'll never divorce his wife—their families have too much jointly invested in

Hawk Hotels to brook a rift...not to mention the fact that she's a staunchly conservative Catholic. If anyone is going to suffer from this liaison it certainly isn't going to be the Hawkwoods...' Simon paused hopefully. Anyone who knew Elizabeth knew that her compassionate heart could always be relied on to support the underdog, even if it sometimes went against her better judgement.

'Oh, Simon...' The exasperated dropping of the respectful 'Uncle' signalled her annoyance as well as her capitulation.

Elizabeth's uncle wisely hid his grin of relief as he tucked the envelope into her reluctant hand and wound the camera strap through the loop of her shoulder-bag.

'Thanks, honey, I knew you wouldn't let me down. Now, hadn't you better check in before the plane takes off?'

He hustled her off towards the desk at a speed that suggested he was afraid she might change her mind, but before they got there he stiffened and stopped in his tracks, dragging her around in front of him.

'What's the matter?'

'Hawkwood. He's over there. Behind you. At the first-class check-in for Air Caledonie.' By slumping his shoulders her brawny Uncle Simon suddenly metamorphosed himself into the shuffling stance of an elderly man rather than the fifty-five-year-old he was. Elizabeth couldn't help admiring the chameleon-like disguise as she automatically began to turn.

'No, don't look now!' Her uncle grabbed her shoulder to stop her. 'He mustn't see us together. Just stand in front of me as if you're saying goodbye...'

'I need to know what he looks like if I'm going to be spying on him,' Elizabeth pointed out drily, and the old man before her frowned.

'There's a photo of him in the file. Whatever you do be discreet, be casual. I'm going to walk away in a minute; you can take a look at him then. You won't be able to miss him. He's the arrogant one in the brown coat with the long black hair and the earring.'

'*Earring*?' Elizabeth was startled.

'It's apparently a Hawkwood male tradition,' her uncle shrugged dismissively. 'Something to do with some Renaissance ancestor and an old superstition about the Hawkwood luck. They seem to have a lot of it and they guard it fairly jealously.'

Elizabeth was dying to look around by now. 'What about her—your client's wife? Is she with him?'

'Serena. Serena Corvell. She flew up this morning, I guess so her husband wouldn't see Hawkwood and start to ask questions.' He proceeded to tell her a few other things that he thought she ought to know and gave her some last-minute instructions and reassurances.

When he was gone and Elizabeth turned around her eyes had instantly found the arrogant man whom her uncle had said she couldn't miss.

He was third in line at the check-in desk, frowning fiercely after a rapidly retreating figure in a dark coat whom Elizabeth ignored, assuming that it was some minion who had delivered His Highness to the airport and managed in the process to annoy him in some way. She had been shocked by the pony-tail and surprised at the sight of jeans beneath the stylish brown trench coat he wore, but, not particularly fashion-conscious herself, she presumed that even millionaire businessmen were glad to get out of suits on occasion, and J.J. Hawkwood was obviously in a sartorial class of his own. She had nervously made her way to the adjacent queue and embarked on her trail of minor catastrophes.

Someone rattled the toilet door now and Elizabeth reluctantly acknowledged that she had lingered as long as she could. She put her sunglasses back on and practised an enigmatic expression in the mirror.

Neither J.J. Hawkwood nor her own fears were going to defeat her. To do a great right it was often necessary to do a little wrong. From now on discretion would be her watchword.

Elizabeth Lamb: undercover operative!

CHAPTER THREE

ELIZABETH slipped back into her seat and re-fastened her seatbelt, saying primly as she did so, 'Thank you for the loan of your shirt.'

'My pleasure,' J.J. Hawkwood murmured, studying her dignified expression with a veiled amusement. 'It suits you far better than it ever did me.'

She was unnerved by the faint hint of possessiveness in his amused look, and Elizabeth's blood boiled at the facile compliment.

She muttered a frosty reply and looked for her magazine to rescue her from any further conversation. To her frustration she realised she must have left it in the front pocket of her economy-class seat. She couldn't even sneak a peak at the file Uncle Simon had given her, not with the subject sitting right beside her.

'Perhaps, since you're wearing my clothes, we ought to introduce ourselves.'

His silky suggestion sent a wave of panic thrilling through Elizabeth's veins.

'I think the hostess has already taken care of the introductions, Monsieur Hawkwood.' Goodness, she sounded even prissier than ever, but she didn't know how else to discourage idle conversation.

Wrong move.

'So she has, Miss Lamb,' he replied equably, but the spark in the silver eyes suggested that he found her evasion annoying and—more dangerous for her—slightly intriguing.

'The hawk and the lamb—a curious coincidence, wouldn't you say? In the wild we would be natural enemies...' His mouth curved in a thin, predatory smile and Elizabeth was hard put to it not to shiver at the appropriateness of his idle musing.

'Yes, I suppose we would,' she said steadily, suddenly remembering the thick instruction booklet that came with the camera Uncle Simon had given her. She fished it out of the camera bag with an inward sigh of relief. Now she had a substantial excuse to ignore him. It would take her a long time to plod through the whole thing—longer if she also intended to try to actually *comprehend* what she was reading.

'New camera?'

Elizabeth gritted her teeth. For some reason J.J. Hawkwood was determined to thwart her attempts at aloofness. Was it his wounded vanity? Would he keep pestering her until she paid him the kind of attention he was obviously used to receiving from women? She wouldn't have thought his ego would be so insecure.

'Yes—I mean, no... it's borrowed—from a relative.' Her hands tightened on the cover as she realised that she was telling him more than he needed to know. Stick to minimal answers, Beth!

He leaned towards her to look over her shoulder at the print, close enough for her to inhale the crisp, clean male scent of him, unmasked by cologne. 'Interested in photography?'

In her nervous state she almost snapped out the truth. Just in time she remembered the image she was supposed to be projecting. 'It's a hobby of mine.'

'Oh, really? What kind of camera do you normally use?'

Oh, God, had she unknowingly blundered on to one of his own interests? Elizabeth lowered the booklet, completely rattled by now. She must try and convince him that she was utterly dull and boring and quite undeserving of any further interest.

'When I said hobby, I meant that I like to have lots of pictures as permanent mementoes from my holidays, that's all,' she told him in a monotone.

'Where exactly in New Caledonia are you spending your holiday?'

Elizabeth stared at him, cornered. If she tried to avoid answering he really would get suspicious. 'Isle of Hawks,' she admitted stiffly, her voice sinking to its natural level.

His eyebrows rose. They were thick and dark and extremely eloquent, expressing a speculative amusement. 'Alone?'

'Yes.' The clipped reply was a terse warning which he blithely ignored.

'And what are you looking to find on your solitary holiday...peace and quiet? A place to relax? Or are you looking for something more exotic...excitement, glamour, romance—a lover perhaps...?'

His outrageousness destroyed her intention to bore him into silence, guilt adding to the intensity of her outburst. 'It's none of your damned business what I'll be doing!'

She went pale when he laughed.

'In the circumstances I think it is.'

'What circumstances?' she demanded raggedly, wondering whether she had blown her cover already.

'Why, that you're a guest of mine, of course,' he said smoothly. 'I would be a poor host indeed if I didn't attempt to find out whatever it is people come to my island looking for, and do my best to provide it for them.'

'Surely you don't have to conduct the surveys yourself. Don't you have employees to attend to those petty details for you?' Elizabeth began. Employees like Serena Corvell!

'It's my attention to petty detail that has made Ile des Faucons one of the finest resorts in the world,' he said with an arrogance that took her breath away. As if the people who lived and worked at the place played a lesser part in its success than the corporate head who paid only flying visits when he could fit it into his busy schedule . . . and then only when he was combining it with an adulterous affair!

'So . . . what is *your* heart's desire, Miss Lamb?'

'Nothing that I require *you* to supply,' she said crisply.

'You sound very sure of that.'

'I am.'

'You're very independent,' he commented. Elizabeth knew that it wasn't supposed to be a compliment. What he really meant was that she was independent of *him*. He obviously didn't like the idea of any woman being beyond his control.

'Well, I hope for the sake of my hotel's reputation that you're wrong. I would hate you to leave Ile des Faucons feeling—*unfulfilled* . . .' His accented drawl was pleasant enough but Elizabeth didn't think that she imagined a touch of angry impatience there. Good. She had finally succeeded in routing his interest.

'Actually, I suppose there *is* something I want that I'm hoping you can provide,' she said impulsively, goaded to consolidate her victory.

'Oh?'

Her small bow of a mouth unravelled into a smile of malicious sweetness. 'Solitude.'

In the ensuing silence Elizabeth returned her attention to her neglected manual, her heart thudding uncomfortably. She really shouldn't have made that last comment but it was his fault. If he weren't an unprincipled lecher she wouldn't be in this thoroughly disturbing situation. Now, she hoped, he would sulk to himself. She knew the type.

In her mind she had already lumped him with the 'fearful few'—those wealthy, spoiled male university students who, over the years, had made the mistake of thinking that wining and dining their professor's researcher would flatter her into spilling the beans on the contents of the latest test paper which they had been too busy socialising to study for.

Men who were used to getting whatever they wanted when they wanted it were generally ungraceful losers, but Elizabeth always took their sullenly assumed indifference as a more genuine compliment than their easy flattery.

When the air hostess brought her a replacement glass of champagne Elizabeth sipped it only cautiously and refused the offer of wine when lunch was served a short time later, aware that she had been too on edge to eat any breakfast that morning. The last thing she needed now was to get tipsy. The food was delicious, elegantly presented in lavish servings which Elizabeth normally would have found no difficulty in enjoying. However, the nerves in her stomach were in no mood to relax and she found she could only nibble here and there—another reason for her to resent the man beside her, calmly devouring every crumb on his plate.

Time seemed to pass with excruciating slowness. Elizabeth pointedly bent her head back down over the camera manual when the lunch dishes were cleared away and fortunately her hint was this time accepted without comment. Placing the earphones over his head and selecting a recorded channel, J.J. Hawkwood reclined his seat even further and stretched out with his eyes closed.

Gradually, as Elizabeth became certain from his slow, even breathing that he was indeed asleep, and, envying him his repose, she dared study him.

With the earring on the ear facing away from her, the flamboyant pony-tail tucked beneath his head and the brutally masculine features relaxed he didn't look half as threatening to her peace of mind. The power of those coldly penetrating, cynical grey eyes was extinguished. Relief surged through her, soothing her fraught nerves. He was just a man, like any other. She mustn't allow his unexpected appearance to shake her resolve. Granted the task she had to perform regarding him was not one she would have chosen to do, or one that she felt entirely comfortable with but, as Uncle Simon had pointed out, Hawk Hotels had its own corporate security staff so J.J. Hawkwood himself had probably taken advantage of similar surveillance reports in the course of his various business dealings.

What incredibly dark hair and eyelashes he had. Both were thick and glossy, the blue-black eyelashes forming lush crescents just above his high cheekbones. There was not a strand of grey to be seen and the shadow along his smoothly shaven jaw was as singularly dark as his head. Did he dye his hair? Uncle Simon had said that Hawkwood was thirty-eight, and it was unusual for a man of that age in such a stressful position of authority not to show a bit of distinguished grey. The harsh angles of his face, while strong and vital, certainly weren't youthful, but there was little other physical evidence of ageing.

Elizabeth looked at his thin mouth, controlled even in sleep, and wondered what sort of woman Serena Corvell was to put herself at his mercy. She had a very powerful urge to look at the envelope in her bag, but she decided that, with the way her luck was currently running, he would wake up and catch her red-handed.

Ruefully she conceded that many women would find the combination of raw physicality and cynical charm irresistibly attractive, especially allied as it was with money and power, but Elizabeth's one brush with reckless love had convinced her that passionate physical attraction was an inherently unstable and completely unreliable indicator as to the depth of one's genuine feelings and the worthiness of one's partner.

Of course she wasn't totally unaware of the brutal sex appeal of the sleeping man—she *was* still a woman—but she felt protected by her shrewd assessment of his unsympathetic character. He would be hell on wheels to love. Poor Serena Corvell.

Elizabeth wrenched her eyes off the sleeping man, deciding that she was brooding far too much on what didn't concern her. Heavens, she had much more important things to think about than feeling sorry for a foolish woman who had fallen in love with an accomplished rake.

The old-fashioned word made her smile. But then, she was an old-fashioned girl in many respects. If she hadn't cared about things like love and honour, respect and loyalty she wouldn't be here now.

Cautiously Elizabeth leaned towards the window, wondering if she would be able to see the sea through the clouds that flitted past the window. There was plenty of blue down there, but was it sea or sky? She thought she glimpsed a thin white arc that could have been a coral reef and as she leaned further across the sleeping man to see it the plane suddenly shuddered and plunged sickeningly before levelling out again. The hand on which she was leaning slid violently off the arm of the seat and skidded down between two relaxed male thighs.

Elizabeth instantly tried to snatch her hand back but was appalled to discover that the gold chain looped several times around her wrist had somehow become entangled in the buttons of J.J. Hawkwood's fly. Of course, he *would* be wearing expensive original Levis 501s instead of the common-or-garden zip variety!

The breath hissing through her teeth in embarrassment, Elizabeth twisted and yanked at her captive hand, but the chain, though thin, was strong.

'Whatever you're doing, *chérie*, don't stop... but please, be gentle with me...'

Elizabeth froze, her eyes fleeing to his face. He was wide awake and watching with interest her delicately frantic struggles with his fly.

She refused to blush. He must know damned well that her actions were totally innocent. She fixed him with her most haughty stare, somewhat ineffectual behind her dark glasses, and said in the deep, authoritative voice that made students cringe, 'My bracelet is caught.'

'Perhaps if you kept your hands out of men's jeans it wouldn't happen.'

She gritted her teeth. 'I was looking out the window. The plane hit an air pocket and I fell. It was an accident.'

His eyes fell to the hand trapped intimately across his lap. 'Really?' he murmured, as if he didn't believe her.

Arrogant jerk! 'Look, are you going to help me or not?' On second thoughts that was a silly thing to say. The blush she had valiantly held at bay overwhelmed her as she waited for the retaliation that she was sure would be mockingly provocative. He seemed to enjoy flustering her. Why, Elizabeth couldn't fathom.

'What do you suggest?' He was still studying her soft, pale hand with its short, unvarnished nails. Her wrist was caught against the placket of his jeans while her hand arched up, straining not to touch the taut denim where it pulled across his loins.

'Just——' She wasn't quite game to ask him to unbutton his fly so she said hastily, 'Just untangle the chain. I think the catch must have got looped around a button because I can't find it . . .'

'So it did,' he said blandly, and, as if divining her thought, calmly began undoing the flat metal buttons on his jeans, watching her fleeting expression of shocked fascination swiftly superseded by one of conscious distaste.

Anxiously Elizabeth began to try and work herself free, only to have him clasp her wrist firmly and hold it until she stilled her premature movements.

'You're only compounding the problem. Don't be in such a rush——'

'Then hurry up!' she spat at him.

'*Chérie*, believe me, the slower you take these things the better it will be——'

'Who for, you or me?' she was driven to snap in a furiously sarcastic undertone. She was acutely aware that just under her hovering palm was the most masculine part of his anatomy, and she had no intention of discovering whether this ridiculous incident was having any physical effect on him. Her imagination, however, was not so easy to control.

He stopped what he was doing, still holding her wrist with one hand. 'Why, Miss Lamb, whatever are you suggesting?'

He was laughing at her. The mouth was still a thin, straight line but she knew that inside he was roaring. Elizabeth had never been more grateful for the dark glasses. She was very close to bursting into tears of fury and distress.

'Just shut up and *do* it!' she begged him, aware, too late, of a presence in the aisle behind her half-turned back, speaking simultaneously with her hushed outburst.

'Would you like another glass of—oh! Uh—perhaps I'll come back a little later...' The air hostess backed hastily away and now the awful man let his amusement conquer him completely.

'You can put that one in your record book,' he grinned widely. 'You actually made an air hostess blush.'

'*I* didn't, you did!' she accused him viciously.

He lifted both his hands, palms out, still grinning. 'If you think you can do better, Miss Efficiency, go ahead. Do it yourself.'

She almost did. She was that furious. However, one glimpse of indecent silky white bikini briefs topped by a smothering of curling dark hair through the denim gap changed her mind.

She turned her head away and after a moment he resumed his measured movements without comment. It seemed to take an awful long time but Elizabeth didn't trust herself to make an issue of it. He was surprisingly gentle as he manipulated her wrist and didn't once brush her unwilling hand against himself as she half expected him to, given the relentlessness of his taunting. With a soft grunt of satisfaction he finally released her.

'I don't think there's any damage, but you'd better check.'

For a moment she thought he was talking about himself, then she realised he meant her bracelet. She concentrated on it fiercely while he readjusted his clothing.

'OK?'

'Yes. Thank you.' She sounded sullen but she couldn't help it. The man was a jinx. 'I hope I didn't damage your jeans.'

'You obviously don't watch the TV ads. It takes more than a lady in distress to wreck a pair of Levis,' he murmured.

At least he had called her a lady and not a klutz. Elizabeth felt her poker spine soften a little. 'I'm sorry, I wasn't very polite——' she began tightly.

'I didn't give you any reason to be.' He disconcerted her yet again by overriding her humiliated apology with a graceful confession of his own. He almost sounded—heaven forbid—*gentle*! 'My sense of humour is sometimes incomprehensible, even to myself. I'm afraid I'm also liable to be crudely direct at times, especially when I'm taken by surprise—my old army instincts surfacing: shock tactics—react first, ask questions later.'

Elizabeth murmured something meaninglessly polite in exchange. Army? Hardly the sort of training she would expect for a wealthy businessman. Perhaps he had been liable for some kind of National Service. Did New Caledonia *have* an army? Her curiosity was becoming perilously close to personal. Resolutely determined not to indulge it, it was Elizabeth's turn this time to recline her seat and close her eyes.

She wouldn't sleep a wink, of course, but she was bound and determined to pretend to be unconscious for the rest of this wretched journey!

A faint buzzing in her ears roused her. She shifted herself restlessly, nuzzling her cheek and mouth contentedly against the soft, warm fabric which pillowed her.

Soft? Warm?

Elizabeth's eyes flickered open. A few inches away another pair of eyes watched her struggle out of her fitful doze. The pillow that she was using was a masculine shoulder. The warmth moulded to her side from head to hip was pliant muscle. The buzzing was the faint electronic beep of the watch on his wrist, which was anchored to his broad chest by Elizabeth's lax hand. The arm-rest which should have bolstered the division between their almost fully reclined seats had been folded out of the way, to all intents and purposes creating a double bed!

Elizabeth had wanted to keep J.J. Hawkwood under surveillance, but not this close!

She pushed herself upright, brushing her ruffled hair back from her hot face with a trembling hand, and looked down at the man lying beside her.

'I'm sorry, you should have pushed me away,' she said huskily, astounded to find that she had relaxed enough to fall asleep. She could have sworn that she had only closed her eyes a few seconds ago but, glancing at her watch, she saw that nearly an hour had passed since she had laid her head down. The tension and worry of the past few weeks had caught up with her at the most inappropriate of times.

'I didn't want to wake you up. You looked as if you needed the rest. The nap did you good—you've gained some healthy colour.' He reached up and touched her flushed cheek with a smoothing caress, as if he had every right to, as if he actually *cared* about the state of a stranger's health. Elizabeth froze and his hand fell back down on to his chest.

'I—I have naturally pale skin,' she muttered.

'You have very unusual colouring. I thought your hair was black at first but it's not, it's a very rich, dark mahogany.' He folded his arms behind his head, his body language suggesting frankness, a complete lack of self-consciousness, a direct contrast to Elizabeth's humming awareness that only a few moments ago she had been cuddled against his side.

She blinked at him slowly, her thoughts still in disarray.

He smiled, not his former taunting smile but one of rare warmth. 'Are you always this sluggish when you wake? Your eyes are as big and sleepy as an infant's. I'm sorry my alarm woke you, but we're due to land in a few minutes anyway. Once we get home you can get some proper rest in a bed . . .'

We? Home? *Bed*? A small shock quaked through Elizabeth's system at the disturbing juxtaposition of words.

Her eyes? Suddenly she realised the import of his other comment. She put a hand to her face and discovered that her sunglasses must have fallen off while she slept.

Or had been deliberately removed. She stopped searching and eyed J.J. Hawkwood suspiciously as he returned his seat to its upright position and produced her sunglasses from his left breast-pocket.

'You were so restless that I was worried you might damage the frames,' he said, handing them over.

Elizabeth debated whether to put them back on and decided that she might as well, although it was a bit like shutting the stable door after the horse had bolted. However, she still needed a defensive shield between herself and her quarry.

'Thank you.' She fiddled with the arm-rest, trying to fold it back where it belonged—a safety barrier between them.

'Again—my pleasure, *mademoiselle*.' With a simple movement he accomplished the deed for her, then watched her grimly struggle to return her seat to its upright position, all thumbs under his regard. He was well named, she decided. He was as watchful as a hawk.

'You don't seem to be having much luck today, do you?' he commented when she finally succeeded in her task. She frowned at him, her brow crinkling beneath her ruffled fringe, and he added suavely, 'We're coming down through the clouds now; would you like to swap seats so you can watch the landing?'

'I'd rather not,' she said uneasily, noting the tilt of the wing and the ragged sweep of wispy cloud which suddenly cleared to reveal a mountainous terrain rotating sickeningly below.

'There's no need to be afraid——'

'I'm not afraid!' Unconsciously her hand had clenched on the arm-rest.

'Is this your first flight?'

'Yes.' She felt hopelessly naïve admitting it.

'First time out of New Zealand?'

Now she felt even more naïve. 'Yes. But I'm not afraid,' she reaffirmed, more to herself than to him.

'Just nervous, hmm? I know the feeling. Even seasoned travellers like me are a touch tense during take-offs and landings...'

Elizabeth hardly heard his soothing murmur; her anxious gaze was riveted out of the window. They seemed to be coming awfully low and she could see nothing but mountains and valleys. Not a sign of any flat or inhabited land. The plane wheeled even further and now she could see the sea where it met a reddish-brown strip of marshy shore. It seemed to go on forever. She had known that New Caledonia was the third largest island in the South Pacific after New Guinea and New Zealand, but still she had somehow imagined a flat coral atoll surrounded by sea. Instead she was seeing a bush-covered volcanic terrain that looked like the edge of a huge continent. The occasional dwelling dotted the landscape but still she could see no sign of an airport and they were coming even lower, the engines roaring and vibrating, setting her teeth on edge. Surely they had been circling far too long?

'I hope the pilot's not lost,' she muttered, swallowing nervously and feeling her ears pop. 'I thought the airport was at Nouméa but I don't see any city...'

'Tontouta is only a very small airport but it's well signposted.' The faint mockery in his tone was more reassuring than his gravity would have been. A warm, abrasive palm closed over her clenched hand, holding it with a firm, confident pressure, absorbing some of her tension. 'It's also about forty-five minutes' drive from Nouméa itself so you won't be seeing the city for a while yet. The travel agents who handle our bookings are supposed to provide a travel package with all that kind of information. Didn't you get one?'

Elizabeth bristled at the hint of criticism. If he knew what she had been going through he would realise why she had been unable to anticipate her holiday with any real enthusiasm! 'Yes, but I haven't read it in detail,' she said coolly, her galloping heartbeat slowing a little as she saw a wind-sock waving in the wind below and a segment of wide black tarmac.

She closed her eyes at the moment of impact, the large masculine hand tightening over hers, the blunt fingers sliding between her own, distracting her from the fluttery anxiety in her stomach. For a man who lived the good life, J.J. Hawkwood had surprisingly work-roughened skin.

'I'm glad *that's* over!' she breathed when the plane finally taxied to a halt. For a moment she forgot that she was supposed to be tough and independent. 'I hate doings things for the first time,' she said shakily.

'That must cast a rather restricting influence over your life,' he commented drily, and she pulled her hand out from under his, her skin tingling at the sandpaper friction of his roughened palm. 'I'm surprised, in that case, that you should choose to travel overseas for the first time alone...'

'I didn't exactly *choose*...at the last minute my friend couldn't come,' she informed him, reluctantly answering the unspoken question.

'What a shame. Is she ill?' The silver-grey eyes were brimming with a heartily offensive innocence.

Her mouth compressed into a starched bow. 'What makes you think it was a *girlfriend*?' she demanded tartly.

The silver gleam intensified and she instantly regretted providing him with the opportunity for more of his exquisite mockery. 'Because you hate first times?' The questioning inflexion was purely for effect.

The prim pink bow lost all its starch as Elizabeth's mouth melted open. How dared he?

'What makes you think I've never been away with a man?' she snapped, choosing the least embarrassing of his slew of implications to fight back on.

'Have you?'

She was too angry to care about the truth. 'Dozens!'

'Singly or in groups?' he enquired with interest.

'Both!'

'Well, all I can say is that you wear incredibly well. That peach-soft skin and those big innocent eyes don't show a trace of your dreadfully dissipated lifestyle. In fact, if I had been asked to guess, I would have said that you were a quiet, shy, respectable lady—a librarian or school-teacher perhaps—who lives with her cat and her books and enjoys quiet evenings at home with friends...'

In other words a boring, sexless spinster. In spite of all her efforts to bring him round to just that point of view Elizabeth was chagrined by the accuracy of his description. Instead of feeling pleased that her disguise had worked she found herself wondering if it had been a disguise at all. Minus the cat and the shyness his guess was infuriatingly close to reality. Only, Elizabeth told herself, she wasn't inhabiting reality right now. She was in a weird topsy-turvy world where the truth was that the boring spinster was a woman of mystery, of secrets beyond his imagining. Yes, the last laugh was definitely Elizabeth's, even though she would never have the satisfaction of laughing out loud.

Acutely conscious that if she fell into the trap of arguing with him she would only compromise herself even more, Elizabeth put her nose in the air and bustled off the plane with the rest of the first-class passengers, ignoring the softly mocking laughter that chased her angry ears.

The open-air staircase which had been rolled over to the door of the plane gave Elizabeth her first experience of foreign climes. It was midday and the sky which she had half expected to be the same azure-blue that had appeared on all the travel brochures was almost as grey and overcast as the Auckland skies she had left behind. But instead of being chilly and damp the air was deliciously warm, the breeze that ruffled her hair was balmy and pleasant, fragrant with a cluster of scents that she couldn't identify.

It was only after she had gone through the immigration check and was dragging her suitcase off the luggage carousel in the small arrivals hall that she suddenly remembered her blouse. In her hurry to get off the plane she had forgotten to seek out the air hostess who had promised to return it to her.

As she turned anxiously to look for a member of the airline staff she caught sight of J.J. Hawkwood. He was speaking to one of the customs officials over by the doors to the street, zipping up the soft brown leather bag which he had opened on the counter between them and hefting it in his left hand. Elizabeth knew that she didn't have any time to waste. Her nerves were already in a sufficiently bad state. If she wasted time trying to find her blouse now she might be forced to walk through the 'No Declarations' channel of the customs check alone instead of surrounded by a comfortable number of the hundred or so other passengers. If a customs officer so much as murmured a polite welcome to his country Elizabeth was afraid she might crack.

The air hostess knew her destination, knew who J.J. Hawkwood was—Elizabeth would wait until she was safely on the Ile des Faucons to try to retrieve her property and return his. The resort was providing coach transport to Nouméa and then a boat out to the island, so in spite of her intention to avoid direct confrontations with her quarry from now on Elizabeth decided that she would casually mention it to him in passing, so that he didn't think she was trying to steal his shirt.

She might be an accessory after the fact to theft but she was not a thief!

Unfortunately, safely out on the pavement, Elizabeth saw the powerful dark-haired figure of J.J. Hawkwood striding not towards the cluster of courtesy coaches provided by the various hotels and resorts, but in the opposite direction, towards a car park. For a moment Elizabeth was disconcerted, then she realised that it was unrealistic to expect that a corporate head would travel by coach, no matter how well appointed. Of course he would be met, possibly by a chauffeured limousine.

But what if it was Serena Corvell he was being met by? What if he and his mistress were going to spend their holiday together somewhere other than the Isle of Hawks? What if the booking at the resort was just a blind and they were going to disappear to some secret love-nest?

Elizabeth dithered for precious seconds before she decided she had no choice but to grab a taxi and follow him. Even if she found out nothing more than the bare fact of their destination at least she could go home and truthfully say that she had done her best.

No one had to know that she was fervently hoping that her best would not be good enough!

CHAPTER FOUR

'MISSED the boat, Miss Lamb?'

Elizabeth closed her eyes briefly. She would recognise that whisky-and-honey voice anywhere, the dark resonances of tone overlaid with a mocking precision that she had encountered for the first time only a few hours ago.

She pivoted slowly on the wooden pier, away from the dark-haired young man on the boat tied alongside.

J.J. Hawkwood, for all the mockery in his voice, wasn't smiling. Although he was still wearing his jeans, his blue shirt was now replaced by a white T-shirt which emphasised the tanned face and heavily muscled arms.

Sweat trickled down between her shoulder-blades under her shirt—*his* shirt. In the time that she had lurked around the marina waiting for the reappearance of her quarry the thickly overcast skies had cleared to the crisp blue of the tourist brochures and the temperature had steadily risen.

'Yes,' she admitted reluctantly, resenting the necessity of making herself sound like a fool in front of him. 'I was just finding out if there was some other way of getting over to the island.'

Her English was as clipped as his. The fact that he was wearing white boat shoes rather than the polished brown leather he had been wearing earlier explained why she hadn't heard him approaching. She hoped he hadn't been behind her long enough to hear her bargaining with the boat-owner in his own language.

His head tilted towards her suitcase at her feet, and the dark brows shifted into a frown.

'Your luggage, too? Didn't the staff on the bus check you all on board the boat?'

The censure in his voice warned her that someone's job might be in jeopardy if she didn't at least come partially clean.

'I . . . I wasn't on the bus. I took a taxi.'

This time his eyebrows rose and he shifted so that she got a good look at the narrowed grey eyes.

'Did you not realise that your reservation included airport transfers?'

'Yes, of course. But I wanted to see a bit of Nouméa before I . . . I left for the island . . .'

In truth, in the hour's trip from the airport she had hardly noticed the scenery, except to note that none of it seemed wildly exotic. The only features that impinged on her nervous anxiety were the deep redness of the earth where it was scraped bare by agriculture and erosion, and the towering flax-like palms with neatly interwoven leaves that reminded her of French plaiting.

Most of her attention had been focused on the fast-moving red Pantera that they were following and which the taxi driver, not surprisingly in view of the importance of the man and the distinctiveness of his car, had immediately identified. Rather than being suspicious of her reasons for following the famous—or notorious—J.J. Hawkwood, the driver had been amused and faintly pitying.

It had soon become irritatingly obvious that he had pegged Elizabeth as the victim of a jealous passion and he had even gone so far as to suggest a short-cut to her quarry's most likely destination—Monsieur Hawkwood's *pied-à-terre* at Port Plaisance. Elizabeth had refused, and when, sure enough, they had skirted the Baie de L'Orphelinat to pull up outside a small but exclusive-looking shopping centre next to a marina she had paid the driver off with less than good grace, after extracting the information that the regular launch service to Ile des Faucons left from the other side of the marina.

The Pantera had disappeared between some tall salmon-coloured buildings perched on the very edge of the dock and the taxi driver, with a sly smirk, had pointed out the top balcony of one of the buildings as the 'Hawk's Nest'.

Elizabeth had been sipping coffee in the shopping centre's open-air roof-top bar when the airport bus, which had obviously obeyed the speed limits that the Pantera and taxi had flagrantly ignored, pulled into the marina. She anxiously watched several of her fellow air-travellers escorted to a launch carrying the hotel logo, ready to spring into action if J.J. Hawkwood made an appearance, but there had been no sign of him and Elizabeth had forced herself to stay put, even though watching the launch leave had left her with a panicky feeling of being abandoned.

She filled in some of her idle time looking at the file that Uncle Simon had given her, thinking that the photograph of Hawkwood was a very poor one. His face was turned slightly off-centre, angled lighting throwing up shadows and lines on his face that hadn't been apparent in the even lighting on board the plane. His face also looked fleshier, less aesthetic, and his right ear sported a discreet gold stud rather than the flashy ring. The shot of his alleged paramour, on the other hand, was excellent. Serena Corvell was a cool, beautiful blonde, and from the haughtily complacent expression on her face she knew it!

Elizabeth had assumed that the hotel launch would be back and forth all day, but when she had finally got fed up with watching the empty balcony on the top floor and made her way down to the harbour-master's office she discovered to her dismay that the trip to the Isle of Hawks took much longer than she had assumed and the launch wouldn't be back again until after the New Caledonian 'siesta' that closed all the shops from eleven a.m. until three in the afternoon. The idea of having to wait one more minute, let alone an *hour* was more than Elizabeth could bear. There must be a boat-owner *somewhere* in the marina who would take her over to the island for the right price.

The answer, according to the three she had tried so far, was that the right price was beyond her pocket. Elizabeth was too prudent a businesswoman to look upon Uncle Simon's offer to pay her expenses as a licence for extravagance, and who knew how many wild-goose chases like today's she might have to embark on to keep tabs on the elusive Hawk?

She had just resigned herself to waiting out the siesta after all when her prey had swooped on her unsuspecting back.

'The bus driver *does* have instructions to come via the scenic route,' J.J. Hawkwood said drily, making her realise how long the silence had stretched.

'Yes, well...I like to be independent,' she reminded him.

'But now you are regretting that independence?' he guessed smoothly. 'Because this no doubt *helpful* young man has explained to you that, this being a privately owned island, he has to have official permission to land anyone on the Ile des Faucons—permission which he does not happen to have...'

'Yes, of course,' Elizabeth lied primly, throwing a brief, reproachful glance back at the guilty man on the boat whose unworthy hide she was saving. No wonder the prices she had been quoted were so exorbitant! 'I was just enquiring, that's all. Actually, I thought I'd just look around the shops while I waited for the hotel boat to come back——'

'Unnecessary, Miss Lamb. My own personal boat is leaving for the island in a few minutes. You will travel with us.'

Not can, not may, but *will*. Elizabeth's pride was pricked.

'Thank you, but I prefer to do some shopping——' she began testily.

'It's siesta. The shops are closed.' He picked up her largest bag, hefting its weight with an ease that hardly stirred the thick muscles of his upper arm. For some reason the demonstration of his strength made her more determined to impose her will on him.

'Put it down.'

'I beg your pardon?' The haughty English correctness was as infuriating as ever.

'My suitcase. Could you please let go of it? I can handle it myself.' She reached for it and he jerked it away.

'I'm sure you can. You're a very strapping young lady. But as a gentleman I insist on being allowed the honour of carrying it on board for you.'

Strapping?

Elizabeth felt a star-burst of anger mingle with a treacherous desire to laugh at his subtly provocative insult. He made her sound like a ten-foot-tall Amazon, bulging with muscles and threats to male dominance.

'Carrying it? Oh, is *that* what you're doing? I got the impression that you were holding it to ransom,' she said tartly. 'Your boat doesn't fly the skull and cross-bones, by any chance, does it?'

'You think I look like a pirate?' He tipped his head, smiling, probably flattered by the odious comparison.

'No,' she lied crushingly. 'But you're certainly be-having like one.'

'I'm told that's my principal charm,' he murmured.

'How depressing for you.'

'You think so?' The smile became thinner, less pro-vocative, and Elizabeth knew that she had finally got under that thick skin.

'Pirates are notoriously cold-blooded, violent and amoral. Your other charms must be singularly unat-tractive if those are the ones that people associate you with.'

For an instant something hot and dangerous flashed in the grey eyes and Elizabeth inadvertently took a few steps back. Her mouth went dry when he matched her, pace for pace.

'Why all the hostility, Miss Lamb? You have re-sented me from the first moment we met on the plane. Why?' He spoke very quietly, and was all the more menacing for it.

'I—I'm sorry, I shouldn't have said that,' she said awkwardly, knowing it was true. She had no right to judge him when she only had one side of the evidence.

She took off her sunglasses and looked at him with her chin high, so that he could see she was perfectly sincere. She had never deliberately set out to hurt anybody in her life—until this wretched man had crossed her path.

He looked into her wide violet eyes with their deep, dark centres.

'No, but you did say it. Now you will tell me why.'

Again that *will*. As if the only will operating around here was his.

'Look, I've said I'm sorry——'

'That's not enough.'

She was intimidated, but she wasn't stupid.

'Well, it will just have to do!'

'I don't like mysteries,' he said bluntly, not taking his eyes off her flushed face.

'That makes two of us!' Elizabeth blurted out in exasperation. 'Look, I think it's best if I wait for the hotel launch to come back——'

'You're a very stubborn woman.'

It was an accusation that she was perfectly comfortable with as far as he was concerned. 'Yes.'

'*Independent* and stubborn.'

She angled her chin a little higher. 'Yes.'

'You have a problem dealing with men?'

She flushed at the unexpected flanking attack.

'No, I have no problem whatsoever in dealing with men!' she denied hotly.

He nodded thoughtfully. 'Ah . . . so it is only me?'

'I——' She was almost grateful for the sharp interruption when it came, until she realised its source.

'Jack, aren't you carrying chivalry *too* far? The woman obviously doesn't *want* a lift. She seems quite capable of making her own decisions!'

Elizabeth's attention, which had been solely focused on the male threat looming over her, now skittered to the companion that she hadn't even noticed. Tall. Slim. Blonde and beautiful in a very glossy, sophisticated kind of way.

Serena Corvell.

Elizabeth's defensive indignation drained away, along with her hectic colour.

J.J. Hawkwood and Serena Corvell. Together. And 'Jack'? She supposed it was his nickname.

The camera over her shoulder suddenly felt like a ten-ton boulder, signalling her guilty intent.

'No, of course not.' Hawkwood was casually soothing. 'Well, Miss Lamb—at least let me take your suitcase over to the hotel; that way you won't have to carry it everywhere while you do your "shopping".'

'Uh—perhaps I will come with you after all...' Elizabeth found her voice hurriedly.

'Oh, for goodness' sake——' Serena Corvell was staring at her with an expression of the utmost disdain for her vacillation.

'If... if the offer is still open, of course,' Elizabeth said stiffly.

For some reason J.J. Hawkwood decided to be perverse as he studied her pale face. 'I wouldn't like you to feel pressured into doing something you didn't want to...'

The irony was almost laughable. This whole trip fell into that category!

'No, really, I want to come,' she said quickly, unaware of the thread of panic in her voice which contradicted the false smile on her lips.

'When I said that the shops were closed, I didn't mean the cafés and restaurants. If you like I could recommend somewhere——'

'*No*!' Her deep voice almost tipped over the edge into desperation. If only he would stop looking at her like that! She cleared her throat and continued more calmly. 'No, I think that I'm a little worn out from travelling after all, and I'd rather lunch at the hotel, so if you don't mind, Monsieur Hawkwood...'

For a moment she thought that Hawkwood was going to persist with his perverse offers of alternatives until he had forced her to flatly *beg* for her passage, but Serena Corvell came unexpectedly to her aid.

'So it's settled, then. *Now* can we go, Jack? I would like to get to the island before nightfall!'

He made a soothing response to her brisk sarcasm and then graciously made the belated introduction.

'Serena Corvell, this is Miss...?'

It seemed a defeat to have to say it. 'Elizabeth,' she said sullenly.

'*Elizabeth* Lamb.' His mocking smile acknowledged his victory. 'We travelled together from New Zealand.' He made it sound as if they had had a formal assignation. 'Please, call me Jack—Monsieur Hawkwood sounds so...*proper*. And I bet they call you Beth.'

She would have liked to deny it. Somehow he made the nickname sound gentle, ineffectual, *boring*... It was on the tip of her tongue to tell him that she was a

spritely, dynamic Liz, but she quelled the impulse. She
merely ignored him as the other woman brushed impatiently past her on the narrow decking and began
striding sleekly towards the end of the pier.

Hawkwood bowed slightly to Elizabeth, indicating
that he would bring up the rear, and after hesitating she
reluctantly complied with his silent command.

Having him walk behind her was an unnerving experience. She discovered that she had forgotten how to
move her limbs naturally, her hips and knees stiffening so that she stumbled slightly like a little girl trying
out her mother's high heels.

Hawkwood must have thought so, too, because he
murmured closely enough to send shivers up her nervous spine, 'I can't let you wear those shoes on board.
You'll have to go barefoot. After all the persuasion it
took to get you on board, I don't want to lose you over
the side.'

He might if he knew what she was up to!

'I have some trainers in my bag,' she said gruffly,
and almost tripped again when she saw where Serena
Corvell was leading them.

Le Faucon. Black lettering on the bow arrogantly
proclaimed its ownership. After her initial surprise
passed, Elizabeth had to admit that the vessel was exactly like its owner—handsome and emphatically in-
dividualistic. Elizabeth had pictured a rich man's toy—
a sleek, fast, stylish white launch bristling with every
piece of marine technology known to man. Instead,
what she got was a graceful old wooden yacht whose
gleaming teak deck and highly polished brass fittings
didn't disguise the subtle signs of her considerable age.

There was even a figurehead, but not the usual deep-breasted nymph. It was a hawk, wings swept back against the bow, predatory beak thrust aggressively forward in search of new prey. A pirate's boat.

Elizabeth was unaware that she had halted, until she received a soft nudge behind her knee that set her in hurried motion again.

'Beautiful, isn't she?'

Was he talking about his yacht, or Serena, who was frowning back at them from the deck and still managing to look gorgeous?

Elizabeth pretended to concentrate on taking off her shoes and stepping gingerly down the weather-beaten gangplank. Once on board she felt horribly trapped.

'This way. We'll stow your bag below.'

Elizabeth followed him carefully down the steep companionway. There was a compact galley and two other cabins below, as well as extra sleeping bunks in the fo'c'sle. The cabin that Jack placed her bag in was surprisingly large, and the wood panelling and floor gleamed with the same loving polish that the rest of the vessel showed.

'It would probably be a good idea to change out of your skirt as well as your shoes. When the wind hits our sails you might find your modesty compromised,' Jack told her blandly.

Elizabeth gave him a prim look, although she had every intention of following his advice. 'I'll have your shirt laundered at the hotel before I return it,' she began, fingering the buttons, feeling suddenly very conscious of the wide, comfortable-looking double bunk behind her.

He shrugged. 'In that case you may as well keep it on. Once we get away from the protection of the "Grand Terre"—the mainland—there'll be a fair amount of salt spray on deck. No point in your ruining another clean blouse even before we reach the hotel.' As she opened her mouth to tell him she had no intention of wearing his clothing longer than necessary he continued glibly, 'Unless, of course, you have some *personal* reason for rejecting the most sensible alternative.'

Unfortunately her reason was all too personal. The thought that the silk against her skin had once sheathed his own lean, hard physique was disturbing. Lovers wore each other's clothes... Elizabeth was disgusted with herself for the wayward thought. He was right. The offer was the most practical, and, besides, at the moment she couldn't think of a convenient lie to explain away her deep reluctance to being in his debt even in the simplest of ways.

'No, of course not,' she murmured awkwardly, and when he made no immediate move to leave she abruptly changed the subject. 'How many crew do you employ?'

He regarded her with a hint of puzzlement. 'You do have very odd preconceptions about me, Eliza-Beth Lamb,' he enunciated softly. 'I don't have to employ anyone, I'm quite capable of handling her all by myself. Although it does help to have someone on board who knows how to rig a sail. Ever done any sailing?'

Elizabeth shook her head, deciding to ignore his provocative pronunciation of her name. His remarks explained the roughness of his hands, so different from the pampered softness she had expected from a wealthy executive.

His eyes narrowed to conceal a fugitive gleam in the grey eyes. 'Hmm. I'll have to find some other way for you to work your passage.'

Arrogant pirate! No doubt he expected every woman to fall at his feet just because he was handsome and rich and powerful and . . . *sexy* . . .

'I'm sure I could swab the decks quite efficiently,' Elizabeth replied coldly, thinking that she could very well also swab his mouth out with soap. He was actually flirting with her while his mistress awaited him above!

'Oh, I'm sure I could think of a more comfortable position for you than on your hands and knees,' he murmured, watching her speaking eyes go purple with outrage before he continued almost seamlessly, 'The galley for instance. Would you mind foraging for a snack while I get us under way? Even with the wind behind us Ile de Faucons is about two hours' sailing time away and we're bound to get peckish before then.'

He left while she was still simmering over a pithy reply. The knowledge that he could tie her up into verbal as well as physical knots was galling.

The cupboards in the galley were another salutary lesson on the dangers of pre-judgement. They were stocked not with the expensive luxuries but with plain, practical fare. Cheeses, brown bread and beer were the main inhabitants of the small refrigerator.

As Elizabeth made a selection of hearty sandwiches she could feel the difference beneath her feet. The gentle rock of the boat had become a rhythmic sway and out of the porthole she could see the craft moored in the marina slipping by as they left the harbour.

It took a bit of juggling for her to get the tray of sandwiches and beer up the narrow companionway, along with the camera she had grimly shouldered in order to take maximum advantage of her enforced voyage, but Elizabeth managed it without spilling anything. She had left her sunglasses back in the cabin and the colours of the sea and sky enchanted her with their glittering intensity. Wary of the stability of her new sea legs and keeping a nervous eye on the shifting sails, Elizabeth edged carefully past the raised cabin to the rear deck, ignoring Jack's approving click when he saw the loose white cotton trousers she had teamed with his shirt.

Serena Corvell was reclining elegantly on the padded stern seating, not lifting a manicured fingernail as she watched Jack at the wheel. Although she, too, was wearing flat shoes they were of expensive snakeskin rather than canvas and the lightweight cream trouser-suit accentuating her slim figure made Elizabeth feel like a lumpy street-urchin in comparison. Thank goodness the cotton trousers and loose shirt hid her over-generous lines from those critical brown eyes.

At the moment they were regarding the tray with a seething discontent that Elizabeth instinctively sensed had little to do with what was actually on offer.

'Surely there must be something other than beer to drink? Go back down and find a bottle of wine. White. And make sure it's cold.'

Elizabeth's easy temper simmered at the order, but Jack was there before her. 'Beth isn't a servant, Serena.

She's just as much my guest as you are. If you want something else go and get it yourself.'

Serena glowered but she didn't stir. She poked broodingly at the thick sandwiches. 'I suppose there weren't any knives down there, either. These are like doorsteps. I doubt if I could get one past my lips.'

You would if I shoved it down your throat, thought Elizabeth with unaccustomed savagery. Without a word she removed the tray from under the disdainful nose and offered it instead to the man at the wheel.

'Thanks.' He bit into a brown square with a throaty sound of satisfaction. 'Mmm, you obviously know the way to a sailor's heart. You can work passage in my galley any time.'

Elizabeth told herself the funny hollow feeling in her stomach was merely hunger and selected a sandwich for herself. 'No, thank you, I get enough of that at home.'

'You have a large family?'

'No—there's only me and my two elderly uncles—they brought me up but they were never very clever in the kitchen so when I was old enough I was very glad to take over.'

'Do you work, as well as keep house for your uncles?'

Elizabeth bit her lip as she realised that she was chattering as if she had nothing to hide. If she was a good detective she would be worming information out of *him*, not vice versa.

She muttered an affirmative and quickly asked him about the reef which surrounded New Caledonia, at the same time offering him another sandwich. He seemed easily diverted by the twin distractions, obligingly informing her that the coral reef was the second largest in the world and that it could be seen from the high ridge that divided Ile des Faucons into two distinct halves.

'The reef is one of the reasons for the hotel's fame. The waters around our island are spectacularly good for snorkelling and skin-diving. Have you done either before?'

'No. Although I like swimming.'

'You must try diving, while you're here.'

'Perhaps,' Elizabeth temporised. Snorkelling she thought she could cope with, but skin-diving was a little too radical.

'My mother used to say that.' His smile in profile was only tantalisingly half revealed.

'What?'

'Perhaps. When she wanted to let me down gently, without causing conflict by an outright refusal. She hoped that if she procrastinated long enough I would forget my desire to do whatever it was she didn't want me to.'

'And did you usually?'

'Never.' There was satisfaction in his smile.

Elizabeth was unable to hide her disapproval. 'It's not good for children always to get their own way.'

'I didn't say I got always my own way. I said I never forgot my original desire. I allowed myself to be distracted, but never lost sight of the compromise involved.' His smile tipped cynically. 'To this day I don't like to compromise.'

'Why doesn't that surprise me?' murmured Elizabeth. No wonder he had taken his corporation from strength to strength. He had a determination, a will to win that was more evident with each passing moment, whether it be an argument, a woman, or a company.

That made him a possessive man. What if he found out that Elizabeth was here as the agent of someone who wished to take one of his possessions away from him—his mistress?

To Elizabeth's intense relief her disturbing thoughts weren't given time to ripen into fears. Serena Corvell's pretence of indifference had lasted only as long as it took for her to realise that her behaviour had thrown the field wide open to a woman whom she had formerly regarded as no competition at all. She got up and strolled confidently across the deck to tease Jack into giving her a turn at the wheel, began talking to him in a low voice that made it clear that Elizabeth's presence was superfluous.

Instead of trying to intrude where she obviously wasn't wanted Elizabeth retreated to the cabin to fetch her camera and casually took a few shots of the retreating mainland, the white sandy beaches curving into a sea that was now cobalt-blue under a totally cloudless sky. Just like the brochures, she thought wryly as she swivelled the lens and focused carefully on the couple at the wheel.

Serena Corvell had tied an expensive silk scarf over her sleek blonde head, leaving her flawless face exposed as she leaned closer to hear something of what Jack said. Their faces were nearly touching in profile as Elizabeth clicked the shutter. She felt strangely breathless as she framed another shot, and then another, nervous excitement running through her veins. Serena was laughing now, and Jack briefly put his hand over hers as it shifted on the wheel.

As Elizabeth clicked the shutter again Jack Hawkwood looked casually back at her, the movement undoubtedly blurring what would have been a perfect shot. The smile on his face died abruptly and Elizabeth jerkily turned and took a blind snap of the empty sea. She cursed herself for the betraying swiftness of her move. It would have been less suspicious to just take the shot. Sure enough, when she lowered her camera she could see out of the corner of her eye that he was still looking at her with that hawkish gaze.

A few seconds later he left Serena at the wheel and was offering to take a photograph of Elizabeth for her 'holiday album'.

'Oh, no, really—I prefer to take photos rather than be in them,' she stammered, clutching the camera tightly. 'I—I don't photograph very well, you see——'

'I can see your problem,' Serena's malicious sympathy floated across the deck. 'The camera doesn't flatter the fuller figure, does it? Leave her alone, Jack, you're embarrassing the poor girl.'

So, not only was she fat, she wasn't even a woman. Elizabeth found herself doing a slow burn at the unnecessary spite of the other woman's words. As if Elizabeth would ever be a threat to a sophisticated woman like Serena, for goodness' sake! It was temper, rather than bravery, that prompted her to delay Jack's return to his mistress's side.

'There's a private estate on the island, isn't there, as well as your hotel?'

His hesitation was so slight that she thought she must have imagined it.

'The St Clair estate, yes. What makes you ask?'

'Is it far away from the hotel?' She tried to make her question casual, eyes avoiding his so that he wouldn't see the avidness of her interest.

'Nothing on the island is far from the hotel,' he said drily. 'It's only a few kilometres across.'

Was he being evasive? Or was it her over-active imagination? 'Someone mentioned that the house is worth a look, that it's like a transplanted French château...' Uncle Miles and Uncle Seymour had been very eloquent about the graceful villa in which old Monsieur St Clair resided—when they had exhausted the topic of the priceless book collection which had been the reason for their visit a few months before.

'It's very impressive.'

She took the unenthusiastic reply as uninterest. 'I'll be sure and go and see it, then . . .'

'I'm afraid that's not possible.'

Against her will her eyes darted anxiously to his. 'Not possible? Why not?'

'The estate is out of bounds to hotel guests.'

'Out of bounds, but why?'

'It's a private home, not a tourist attraction. Monsieur St Clair doesn't care for casual visitors.'

Elizabeth was tempted to tell him that she wasn't a casual visitor but she bit her tongue and turned away, pretending to be absorbed by the sight of seabirds skimming the calm wake of the yacht. Discretion must be her watchword, at least until she had had a chance to speak to Monsieur St Clair himself.

Unconsciously she touched the white shirt where it lay concealingly across the heavy, wrought-gold necklace, feeling again the faint chill of the shock she had experienced when Uncle Miles told her the unfortunate aftermath of their buying trip to the St Clair estate. She had known that Uncle Seymour was becoming prone to bouts of increasing eccentricity in old age, but she hadn't realised that his magpie tendencies had developed into something more serious until Uncle Miles had shown her the evidence.

Uncle Seymour might not have actually stolen the necklace personally, but he had certainly kept it in the guilty knowledge that it was someone else's property. Monsieur Alain St Clair's to be exact.

The two crates of books which had been shipped to Lamb's Tales from the St Clair estate had contained, for the most part, the brothers' legitimate and documented purchases. But when Uncle Seymour had unpacked them he had found there were also three valuable first editions apparently included by mistake and an apparently worthless book that had contained, within its hollowed-out pages, the necklace that Elizabeth was now wearing. An antique necklace that was breathtakingly beautiful and obviously extremely valuable. Stamped on to the ornately carved clasp was an unmistakable mark of ownership—the St Clair family crest.

Instead of doing the proper thing and immediately rectifying the mistake Uncle Seymour had tucked away his find in the old roll-topped desk in his room. Uncle Miles had been shattered when, one evening two months later, he had stumbled upon his brother possessively admiring his treasured hoard. Uncle Seymour had been truculent, stubbornly refusing to accede that he had done anything wrong or to perceive any negative repercussions to their business reputation if his actions were made public. He had insisted that he was just 'minding' the books and necklace until their return was requested.

Uncle Miles had worried about the problem for several weeks as he tried without success to contact Monsieur St Clair personally by phone and by letter. The estate staff were brusque and uncommunicative and his letters remained unanswered. It was only when the strain got too much for him that Uncle Miles had reluctantly confided in Elizabeth and asked for her active help in returning the valuable items to their reclusive owner.

'Oh, Monsieur St Clair is still living there, then. He's quite old, isn't he? Is he still in good health?' she asked Jack now.

'Why do you ask?'

'Oh, no reason—I'd heard he was a recluse.'

Every reason in the world. If by any chance the old man was ill and died before Elizabeth got to him then a delicate situation would become extremely dangerous.

On the other hand an illness might explain the reason why there had been no apparent hue and cry about the disappearance of some highly valuable possessions. If the police were not yet involved Elizabeth knew that there was a good chance that she could extricate Uncle Seymour from the folly of his age without any shameful publicity or embarrassing legal red tape. If Monsieur St Clair was old and not in the best of health himself he might be better able to appreciate Elizabeth's plea for forgiveness for her uncle's temporary moral lapse.

Jack Hawkwood was looking at her with that unsettlingly thoughtful gaze again.

'If by recluse you mean does he value his privacy—
yes, he does. Very highly. Hotel guests are expressly
warned against trespassing. If they do, and are caught,
their booking can be terminated forthwith and they will
not be welcome back on the island again.'

'A little drastic, isn't it?' Elizabeth said faintly, appalled at the realisation that she wasn't going to be able
to just walk up and knock on the door, as she had
naïvely assumed she would do.

'But very effective.'

It was a very blunt statement, one that told her that
she would get no more information on the subject out
of Jack Hawkwood.

Not that he had told her anything positively helpful. He might be proving a push-over where getting
evidence of his involvement with Serena Corvell was
concerned, but for the rest she was very definitely on
her own!

CHAPTER FIVE

As ELIZABETH depressed the shutter-release two things happened simultaneously.

A slim, darkly tanned redhead wearing a string bikini draped herself across the viewfinder, totally obscuring Elizabeth's target, and the sun-lounger from which Elizabeth had been precariously leaning in order to get a better shot tipped over.

Picking herself up off the silky white sand, Elizabeth swore under her breath as she smoothed down her loose multi-coloured beach shirt and checked her camera for damage. She righted the sun-lounger, shaking out the huge royal-blue hotel towel before she spread it back on the lounger and sat down again, smiling half-heartedly at the chuckles and amused gibes of the guests in the immediate vicinity. Damn J.J. Hawkwood!

She glared at the subject of her frustration, who was lying further along the beach. The redhead was kneeling provocatively beside him, laughing down into his lazily responsive face, ignoring the discontented expression of Serena Corvell sitting under a sun-umbrella beside him.

The unfaithful wife of Uncle Simon's suffering client was evidently not having the holiday of her dreams. Well, nor was Elizabeth, and she was meanly glad that someone was sharing her disenchantment with this island paradise.

The hotel complex was unlike any Elizabeth had ever seen, a low sprawl of sinfully luxurious bungalows, each sub-divided into two separate suites, and interconnected by paths of crushed shells winding among luxuriant hibiscus, poinsettias and oleander shrubs. The main building, a graceful three-storey structure directly overlooking the curving beach of powder-fine white sand, housed three restaurants, the extensive sports facilities, casino, nightclub and numerous bars. A huge swimming-pool competed with the tranquil turquoise waters of the bay to lure the guests into taking full advantage of the balmy New Caledonia weather.

Elizabeth had been at one of the most fabulous hotels in the world for three days and she still hadn't found time to enjoy herself! If anything her anxieties had increased. Although she had placed the necklace, cleverly sealed in festive paper, in the hotel safe, she had not managed to persuade the hotel telephonist to connect her with the St Clair estate. Off-limits to guests evidently also extended to phone calls.

Her surveillance was also proving a disappointment. From the time that Jack took a morning jog along the beach while Serena breakfasted on the veranda of his bungalow until three or four in the morning when the casino finally closed, the pair were constantly on the move, but they actually seemed to spend little time alone together. Elizabeth was beginning to despair of getting any more 'compromising' photographs than those she had taken on the boat coming over.

She took one now, just for the hell of it. She had a feeling that she could walk up and snap the camera right under their noses and neither Jack nor Serena would pay a blind bit of notice. Their lives were far too self-involved.

Perhaps the lovely Serena was coming to the same conclusion that Elizabeth had reached through the objective magnification of her long lens: that J.J. Hawkwood's excessive sociability with his guests was in the nature of a flashy conjuring trick. In fact, for all his affability, there was a reserve, a wariness about him that drew a definite line between the public and private man, over which few presumed to step.

Certainly, she had discovered to the detriment of her nerves, under that lazy exterior he had fearsome stores of energy to burn.

Sure enough, he wasn't content to lie on the beach for long. A few minutes later he was walking off into the palm trees that lined the beach, hand in hand with the luscious redhead!

At first Elizabeth couldn't believe her eyes. She looked from Serena Corvell's stiff face to the man retreating along the sand. A number of other women on the beach were also openly studying his form.

Elizabeth grudgingly had to admit it was superb. Unlike his thickly furred chest his back was a tapering sweep of smooth bare skin, from wide shoulders to lean hips. His legs were long, slender yet powerful as they flexed with each easy stride. Sprinter's legs and a swimmer's chest—an awesome combination. Stripped to dark blue racing-style swimming-trunks, Jack was impressively male.

But not perfect, Elizabeth saw with a jolt, for down one hair-roughened thigh was a curving scar which reached from hip-joint to knee. The flaw only served to emphasise the perfection of the rest of him.

Ten minutes later, crouched awkwardly behind the massive roots of a banyan tree overlooking a small beach that was scarcely large enough to merit the name, she admitted to herself that she had exceeded her orders by following Jack Hawkwood and his bikini-clad friend, but the woman in her was outraged by his behaviour.

She raised her camera, propping it against one of the gnarled roots. Get on with it! she silently urged as she squinted grimly through the lens. All she needed was a kiss and then she would leave them to their sordid games. Getting a shot of Jack being unfaithful to the woman he was being unfaithful to his wife with was worth compromising her conscience for. If nothing else such a photograph might help bring poor Serena Corvell to her senses!

A cheesecake shot of a half-naked woman standing alone on a beach wasn't what she wanted. Elizabeth lowered the camera, wondering where the other half of her composition had gone. She found him, all too quickly—sprinting up the sand towards the stand of trees where she was hiding. The expression on his face was as hard as the rest of him. In contrast the woman he had left was laughing as she turned to jog off along the beach, back in the direction of the hotel.

Elizabeth turned and ran.

She didn't know whether she had been rumbled or not but she wasn't waiting around to find out. The sandy soil of the island didn't support a thick undergrowth, and Elizabeth knew that she wasn't going to get much cover from the slender-trunked gums and pine trees, so concealment depended on putting as much distance between herself and Jack as quickly as possible. She could hear him behind her, gaining on her. It wasn't coincidence. He might not know who he was after but he was certainly in full pursuit.

Hopelessly disorientated by panic, she stumbled on as fast as she could in her slip-on sandals, hoping for a miracle, knowing that she was being foolish, knowing that he must now be able to see her quite clearly as she darted around the trees.

She screamed softly when she felt the tug on the fluttering tail of her beach-shirt and wrenched away, losing her balance and her shoes simultaneously. She fell, dropping the camera and hearing him hit the ground with an 'oomph' behind her, her momentum carrying her forward, sprawling thankfully out of his reach. She scrabbled desperately along on her hands and knees, preparing to spring to her feet again when she felt a warm iron manacle clamp on her ankle and yank the support from under her. With a soft cry she fell face-first into the sandy soil. She panted and kicked, but to no avail. He flipped her neatly on to her back and literally climbed up her body until he was pressing her down with the weight of his full length, his menacing face a murmur away from hers.

'Well, well, well,' he drawled as she squirmed beneath him, his breath feathering hot and spicy across her angry face. 'If it isn't the lonesome dove. Voyeurism, Beth, is that how you get your kicks...?' There was no surprise in his voice, only a grim triumph. So he *had* known who he was chasing.

'I don't know what you're talking about!' she panted, trying to summon an innocent outrage. 'How dare you? Get off me!'

Her muslin shirt was transparently thin, and underneath all she wore was a plain black maillot. They might as well both be naked for all the protection their beach attire afforded. Elizabeth could feel every muscle in his body, hot and hard and damp from the fever of the chase. Her breasts were painfully crushed by his thick chest and she could feel every breath he took as if it were her own.

Suddenly Elizabeth was very aware of the stillness around them, the soft whisper of the sea, the sandy ground abrading the back of her legs, the snug fit of his hips as they straddled hers.

'Get off!'

This time her gasp was more of a plea than a demand, but of course he didn't move. He just lay there, his grey eyes enjoying her obvious helplessness.

In a last-ditch effort to assert herself Elizabeth reached out and grabbed the neat pony-tail at the back of his head and pulled sharply. The jolt should have brought tears to his eyes but to her horror he didn't even flinch, the corded muscles of his neck hardly registering the sudden extra tension. Instead he smiled faintly and as she jerked her hand away the thin black band that had held his hair in place came with it. His hair loosened across his braced shoulders, slipping caressingly through her retreating fingers like fine, dark silk. A strand fell forward, teasing her parted lips, the feathered tip adhering just inside the moist corner of her mouth.

Elizabeth froze, her eyes dilating with renewed shock as he delicately reached inside her mouth with his blunt fingers to extract the intimate intrusion, brushing the dampened strands tauntingly across her vividly flushed cheek before tucking them safely behind his ear.

'Do you like the way I taste, Beth?'

His mocking murmur was barely discernible through her excruciating embarrassment.

'Get off...please!'

She almost choked on the final word but to her surprise he politely obliged, rolling sideways. When she knelt and tried to get to her feet she discovered the limits of his concession—she was now held by her wrist. He sat up at right-angles to her, one leg drawn up casually to support the arm holding her captive, the other stretched out in front of him. Her ankle still tingled from the power of his grasp and now her wrist began to pulse uncomfortably against the palm of his hand.

'Let me go.'

'Why—so you can seek out another couple to spy on?'

'I wasn't spying.'

'No? You followed us from the main beach...'

Elizabeth stopped tugging at her wrist and tried not to show her dismay. 'Whatever makes you say that?'

'You're not exactly inconspicuous.'

'Why should I want to be?' she countered flatly. 'I was just going for a walk. Why on earth should I want to follow you and your...little friend?'

In spite of her best efforts at indifference some of her scathing contempt leaked out in the last two words.

'Exactly my question. And not only follow us. Take photographs.'

Elizabeth couldn't help her eyes darting sideways towards her fallen camera. Unfortunately it lay well out of reach.

'I happened to be taking photographs of the scenery——'

'And Bunny and I just *happened* to get in the way, hmm?'

Elizabeth was momentarily distracted from her distressing situation. *'Bunny?'* she repeated incredulously.

He shrugged impatiently. 'A nickname.'

'And a very appropriate one, too, I would guess,' muttered Elizabeth cuttingly.

'If you mean that she's cute and soft and cuddly, I'd agree with you,' he replied smoothly. 'But I doubt whether your jealous remark was supposed to be complimentary.'

'Jealous? Why should I be jealous?' Elizabeth's eyes were violet with contempt.

He shrugged again, a fluid movement of his shoulders that sent echoing ripples through the muscles of his arms and chest. 'Maybe you envy her her lack of inhibitions about her body——'

'I'm not inhibited,' she lied. 'Just because I don't choose to flaunt my body at every passing male——'

'Oh, nobody could accuse you of doing that, *chérie*. Your skin is still as pale and delicate as it was when you arrived. You only shed that cover-up when you go in to swim and you don't do that very often in spite of the fact you seem to be something of a water-baby.'

A *frisson* of unease passed through her. Had she been so busy pretending not to watch him that she hadn't noticed *him* watching *her*?

'I don't see any point in going home from a holiday burnt to a crisp, and I'm here to relax, not exhaust myself by swimming marathons.'

'So why aren't you relaxed?' His thumb wandered over her pounding pulse, his eyes wandering over her tense face.

'People relax in different ways,' she said feebly.

'Your way is certainly very different. You're always on the move, aren't you, flitting here and there, taking endless photographs, early to rise and in the casino until the wee hours——?'

'I like being busy!' The irony was that her busyness only reflected his.

'Especially in my vicinity.'

'Look, Mr Hawkwood——'

'It's a bit late for that, Beth——'

'Jack, then. If you'll let me go I'll explain——'

'You'll explain anyway,' he said pleasantly. Without taking his eyes off hers he leaned back and picked up her camera, weighing it in his hand. 'Had any of your film developed yet? I can arrange to have it done for you at a generous discount...'

Elizabeth swallowed. 'No. I'd rather wait until I get home—it's more fun to get the prints done after a holiday is over...'

His eyelids concealed the change of expression in his eyes. 'Of course it is. I just thought that if the photo of Bunny and me was good she might like to have a print...'

'I'm not sure whether I got her in the shot at all, since I was actually framing it much higher, around the two yachts out by the point where the bougainvillaeas are growing,' Elizabeth improvised wildly.

'Mmm.' That enigmatic sound was beginning to get on her nerves.

'May I get up now?' she asked meekly.

In answer he lifted her captured wrist and brushed his lips against the pale marks left by his fingers. 'If you would, I'd appreciate the help.'

'Help?' Unconsciously she rubbed away the kiss as she got slowly to her feet, feeling the threat of pins and needles in her calves, which had been cramped under her for so long.

His mouth pulled sardonically at one corner.

'I'm not as nimble as I used to be in my reckless youth.'

'Forty isn't old,' Elizabeth told him unsympathetically, ignoring the hand he held out, adding an extra two years as a jab at his male vanity.

He tilted his head, and gave her a very dry look. 'Considering I'm only thirty-five, that could be taken as an insult.'

Elizabeth felt ridiculously shocked by the insecurity revealed by the blatant lie.

'It must be your suntan that makes you look older,' she said spitefully.

'Are you going to help me up or not?'

'Maybe at thirty-five you're getting too old to chase women,' she jeered.

'A man is never too old.' He dropped his hand, using it instead to support himself as he shifted himself on to his right hip, wincing slightly as he drew up his straightened left leg—the one with the long scar.

Elizabeth gasped as she realised that she had mis-judged him.

'Are—are you hurt?' she faltered, crouching back down beside him.

'No more than usual.' She could see a fine mist of perspiration forming on his dark brow as he moved the leg again. He was in real pain.

'But your leg——' She broke off, her soft palm hov-ering above the raised scar tissue that seamed the hard thigh, the toughened ridge of skin a smooth pink highway snaking through the dark hair that coated the rest of his leg. An old scar, fully healed, but obviously with some permanent effects. 'What happened? Did you have an operation?'

He stiffened, causing her to recoil both physically and mentally. 'Don't go soft on me now, *chérie*,' he warned savagely. 'I might be tempted to take advan-tage of it. You don't want to ruin a perfect record for infuriating me.'

'Did you hurt it when you fell just now? Perhaps you shouldn't try to get up yet.'

Her sympathy was as unwelcome as her former ret-icence. 'Don't *perhaps* me, Beth,' he growled, remind-ing her of his distaste for the word.

'I'm not your mother!' she reproved him sharply.

His eyes drifted from the anxious tuck of her mouth to the modest scoop-neck of her maillot, exposed by the rolled collar of her shirt, and the generous swell beneath. His smile was a painful parody of a leer. 'Pity. You have such an *abundance* of maternal potential. My mother was rather more under-endowed and chose to bottle-feed. If I'd been suckled by you I'm sure I'd have been the fattest, happiest, not to mention horniest baby in the neighbourhood.'

For a moment she felt like smacking his head off, but her instincts told her that his obscene remark was a deliberate insult, aimed at alienating her sympathy and stifling any further curiosity.

'Don't take your deprived childhood out on me,' she said calmly, standing back up. 'Now do you still want my help or do you just want to lie there and sulk with your injured pride?'

He was slowly working his way around to his knees, his face a rigid mask, his eyes chilled into icy slits. 'Bitch.'

'Ask nicely, Jack, or I'll just stand here and watch you floundering around at my feet. Now that really *would* be entertaining.' At least a dose of his own medicine seemed to be giving him something other than the pain to focus on. 'Perhaps I could go and find Bunny for you. I'm sure she'd love to see macho man gritting his teeth and sweating and swearing and weak as a rabbit himself——'

'Damn it, Beth, I've never begged a woman for anything and I'm not starting now. All I wanted was a hand up, but I'll do it my bloody self——'

'You really should stop swearing, Jack, it's the sign of a limited mind.' She bent and slid an arm across his back, lacing her hand under his arm and taking his full weight as he pushed himself to his feet with his uninjured leg. The only sign that it caused him any pain was a swiftly indrawn breath that reissued on a soft snarl.

'Thank you.'

Elizabeth wasn't offended by the offensive manner of his gratitude. She let him shake off her touch, noticing he was still in possession of her camera as she said self-righteously, 'If you hadn't been so paranoid it wouldn't have happened. You could just have called out to me, you know, instead of scaring me by running at me like a maniac.'

'Oh, is that why you took off like a scalded cat? And there I thought it was a guilty conscience.' His sarcasm was as pronounced as his disbelief. 'As it happened it wasn't the run that did me in, it was the hefty kick you gave me.'

Elizabeth clenched her hands in an effort not to let him see how awful that made her feel. 'I was only defending myself. I thought you were attacking me——'

'What did you think I intended to do? Ravish you?'

His incredulity was well founded, but it only made Elizabeth feel more defensive. 'I don't know. I...I suppose I didn't stop to think.'

'No? It seems to me that *you're* the one suffering from paranoia. The life of a university research assistant must be more thrilling than I imagined.'

Elizabeth's stomach tightened. 'How do you know what I do?'

'The hotel holds your passport.'

'And you looked at it?' Elizabeth paled. The knowledge that his curiosity had extended that far was infinitely threatening.

'It's a perk of the job,' he said sardonically, 'pawing through each batch of passports to see if there's any women worth ravishing.'

'I didn't think you were going to ravish me,' Elizabeth muttered through clenched teeth.

'Oh, good, we're making progress.' While they were talking he had been slowly flexing his injured leg and now he began to massage it.

'Is it feeling better? Will you be able to walk back to the hotel?'

'I won't need a wheelchair if that's what you mean.' He took a few paces back and forth, limping noticeably.

'You must have needed one once,' blurted Elizabeth involuntarily.

'Once.' The acknowledgement was tight with loathing. 'Never again.'

'I . . . I haven't caused any permanent damage, have I?' she asked anxiously.

'I have a high pain threshold,' he said with a grimly reminiscent smile that cut her to the bone. For him to have been in pain she must have hurt him quite badly.

'I'm sorry. I didn't mean to hurt you——'

He shrugged off her apology. 'You just happened to make a lucky strike on an injured nerve, that's all.'

That's all? His casual dismissal only made her feel more culpable.

'Is there anything I can do?'

He stopped his pacing and looked at her, eyes narrowed on her pale face and the expression of unwilling compassion that kept her hovering when she longed to flee.

'Well, you could kiss it better, but I'll excuse you on the grounds that physical deformity at close quarters is something of a turn-off.' The cynical resignation of his black humour was like a shining challenge.

Elizabeth was rarely given to impulse. Instinctive emotional reactions were dangerous. They were unreasoning and usually embarrassing. The one and only real love-affair of her life had been doomed by her over-impulsive passion. As a grown woman she knew the value of thinking before she acted or reacted, which made her spontaneous action now all the more inexplicable.

She sank to a crouch, placing her hands lightly on either side of his thigh for balance as she bent forward and pressed her mouth gently against the site of his injury. Her hair, caught by the breeze, blew in a soft dark froth across his hard abdomen. His skin was hot and faintly salty and her lips parted in inadvertent curiosity over the jagged scar that bisected his outer thigh.

For a stunned second he didn't react. Then, beneath her fingertips, the muscles in his thigh bunched violently and his hand fisted in her hair, wrenching her head back.

'What in the hell do you think you're doing?' he demanded hoarsely, the shock flaring in his silver eyes as he looked down at her.

She was as shocked as he. A wave of colour swept over her pale face, her eyes widening to meet the shattering impact of his.

'I . . .' She sought desperately for a reason to explain away her foolishly impulsive gesture. Had a woman he cared deeply about rejected him because of his scars? Was that the source of his cynicism? His wife, perhaps? Would that explain their estrangement and his subsequent restless womanising?

His hand tightened in her hair, dragging her upright with an ease that belied any remaining physical weakness, holding her still for his perusal.

'I was only joking,' he murmured, staring at the small mouth that had shocked him out of his world-weary indifference.

'So was I,' she lied shakily, trying not to tremble under that probing gaze, desperately wishing she hadn't given in to the fleeting weakness that had assailed her at the thought of his suffering.

'Really?' His shock receded as swiftly as it had come. 'Then here's something else to laugh at...'

His mouth was hot and spicy, aggressive and not at all amusing. He kissed her as though he already knew her mouth intimately, every moist corner and secret crevice, and was merely reacquainting himself with its store of infinite pleasures. His hand threaded deeper into the tangled weave of her hair, tilting her head against his shoulder so that he could brace her against the aggressive plunge of his tongue, filling her so completely with each thrust that she was dizzied by the taste and smell of him. There was a vague thud as he let her camera fall, then his other hand laced with hers, pulling it around his waist, placing it, pressing it there, splaying her fingers over the rippling satin of his back, daring her to explore the bold, restless movement of muscle under skin as his body shifted and rubbed against hers.

Taken off guard by the swiftness of his sensual assault, Elizabeth was ravished by her unexpectedly intense response. It happened so fast that no thought of resistance entered her pleasure-clouded brain; all she could do was flow with the incredible feeling. With a thoroughly uncharacteristic and totally unfounded trust in his masculinity she was sure that she could rely on him to stop before his challenge turned into a full-blooded seduction. After all, they didn't even *like* each other...

The sheer expanse of sun-warmed, faintly gritty naked skin clinging and sliding in delicious friction against hers was intoxicating, a slow, erotic massage of her senses. Then there were the frank sounds of enjoyment that he made, both inarticulate and bluntly explicit, with which he encouraged her to abandon her inhibitions.

When he relinquished her fingers they dug helplessly into his back, afraid to let go of the only stable force in her universe. Her other hand fluttered nervously against the thick bulge of his upper arm until he caught that, too, and drew it into the thick, downy nest of his upper chest, stroking it against himself. Her palm felt the scrape of a stiffened nipple surrounded by the luxurious softness of his body hair and lingered there, exploring the contrast in textures. She leaned further into his kiss, instinctively teasing the tips of her breasts against his silky-hot skin, the astonishing pleasure of it all going straight to her head and making her mouth as aggressive as his.

A deep groan vibrated in his chest, making her tingle all over. His teeth softly savaged her swollen lips. The hips that had been crowding lightly against the juncture of her thighs suddenly ground harder, deeper and Elizabeth became devastatingly aware of the extent of his arousal. Her sense of security vanished like smoke in a mist. Perhaps he wasn't quite as much in control as she had assumed. Her wanton response was probably way out of proportion to what he had expected from a simple kiss. She had reacted as if she were nineteen again, and unable to control her embarrassing sexual impulses.

She must have made a small, distressed sound because he lifted his mouth reluctantly from hers and muttered something in French that made her blush, his hands sliding down over the jut of her buttocks, cupping them tightly, lifting her on to her toes and adjusting her to the hardness between his thighs, holding her there for a long, agonising moment.

'I didn't mean this to happen . . .'

His gravelly words merely confirmed her humiliation. Like Ryan, Jack probably expected a sophisticated rather than clumsily eager response to his lovemaking.

Come to think of it, Ryan had been very similar to Jack—handsome, intelligent, experienced. He, too, had found the voluptuousness of Elizabeth's passion initially arousing but ultimately painfully embarrassing . . . painful to Elizabeth, at least. He had been her first lover and, as a visiting professor of art history, had seemed the epitome of the Renaissance Man to Elizabeth. Only, as it turned out, it wasn't romance but sex that had been the driving force of their relationship.

When she had begun to embarrass him with the frankness of her behaviour Ryan had explained crisply that she was confusing intense physical infatuation with genuine love, that they weren't suited to a long-term relationship because Elizabeth was obviously one of those people who was ruled by her passions whereas Ryan preferred to be in control at all times. She was too . . . *excessive* . . . in her physical and emotional demands on him. She had made him feel stifled. He had even described her as sexually *intimidating*!

Already secretly a little worried by the instinctive ease with which she had accepted sex as a vital part of her everyday life, Elizabeth had been devastated by what she interpreted as a hint that she was a budding nymphomaniac. It was true that her appetite for love-making with Ryan had seemed to be insatiable, but she had thought that the enthusiasm was mutual. She had been so greedily self-absorbed in achieving her own selfish satisfaction that she had failed to notice that she was increasingly the one taking the initiative in their physical relationship.

From this fresh perspective Elizabeth had suddenly seen how appallingly lop-sided her life had become since she had discovered the sexual side of her nature. Her friends had been ignored, her studies taking second place to constant daydreams and fantasies about sex with Ryan. She imagined herself wildly in love with him but she didn't dream about marriage and babies—no, she dreamt about their thrilling encounters in bed!

Thank goodness Ryan had opened her eyes to the dangers inherent in her character while she had still been young enough to consciously change. Without his warning she might have drifted from bed to bed for the rest of her life, wondering why she could never find the satisfaction she restlessly sought, wondering why her lovers always left. As it was she had circumvented the problem by ignoring it. Men as friends were far more enduring when you didn't clutter the relationship with diverse sexual tensions.

'Don't look so horrified; your virtue is still intact.'

The dry words jolted her back to the present. No thanks to her! Another few minutes and she might have thrown him to the ground and had her way with him.

Another horrifying thought struck her. Not only was she guilty of losing her head, she had been tempting a man to adultery. This man was *married*, for goodness' sake; that alone should have made her recoil from his embrace. That she hadn't even considered the taboo was a measure of how perceptive Ryan had been six years ago.

Stiffly Elizabeth disentangled herself from the supporting arms that moments ago she had badly needed.

'Should I apologise?' he had the misfortune to ask softly as she averted her face.

'Not to me. It's just the kind of disgusting behaviour I would have expected from you.' She turned to glare at him accusingly.

'There's nothing disgusting about two people kissing,' he pointed out in mild surprise.

'In certain circumstances there is.'

'Oh? And what would they be?' He looked amused. His mouth was faintly reddened by their sensual encounter and Elizabeth went hot just looking at it.

'If one of the people is *supposed* to be saving their kisses for someone else!'

He shoved a lazy hand through his hair, slicking it back from his forehead to let it fall neatly behind his ears. As straight as it was dark, it framed his long throat and just brushed the thick, tanned shoulders.

'If you mean Bunny, she was a means, not an end. She's a hotel employee. She's paid in francs, not kisses——'

'I meant when you're *married*!'

He went very still. 'You're married?' His eyes flicked down, puzzled, wary. 'You're not wearing a wedding-ring.'

'Not me, *you*!' she cried.

'Whatever makes you think I'm married?' he had the gall to ask innocently.

'Your wife and children, perhaps?' said Elizabeth with sweetly vicious sarcasm.

'What wife?'

'The one in France. The one living on your family estate, with your *children* . . .'

Enlightenment dawned, and suddenly the grey eyes were lit with a mocking brilliance. 'Ah, *that* wife and family. Beth—who do you think I am?'

'Who do I——? I *know* who you are.'

'Humour me. Tell me about my wicked self.'

Infuriated, Elizabeth bent to sweep up her camera and leave, but his reactions were lightning-swift.

'Humour me,' he invited her softly, beating her to it and swinging her camera mockingly from its strap.

'You're Jean-Jules Hawkwood. You own this hotel and about two dozen more all over the world,' Elizabeth gritted at him.

'So why do people call me Jack?' he wondered blandly, slurring the first consonant through his teeth.

'I don't know.' Elizabeth shrugged impatiently. 'I suppose it's just a nickname——'

'Or it could be my actual name,' he drawled.

'I told you——'

'And now *I'm* telling *you*. My name is Jacques. Jean-Jacques Hawkwood. I don't own this hotel. I only manage it. For my brother. My elder brother. Jean-Jules Hawkwood.'

The whispering sea was suddenly a deafening roar in her ears.

'You—you mean you're not——?' she croaked. Her mind went numb as she clutched desperately at straws. 'But—you *must* be... I *saw* you—and—Mrs Corvell... she's here with *you*...'

There was a different kind of stillness about him this time, not of shock but of instant alertness, a brooding suspicion that turned the sunlit grey eyes darkly overcast.

'Serena came as a guest of my brother's, yes—you have *that* information right,' he confirmed slowly. 'But Jules was called away to New York unexpectedly, and since I was in New Zealand at the time I was the natural person to bring the news back to Serena, who had come on ahead, and to help keep her entertained until Jules arrives... *if* he arrives.'

Jack had stopped swinging the camera and instead studied it and her with a menacing interest that sent chills down her spine.

'In fact I swopped my original return flight to Nouméa for Jules's earlier booking, since my Auckland business was concluded anyway. We even went out to the airport together—his plane to New York was taking off half an hour after ours. Maybe that was where you got us mixed up—we look very much alike so I'm told...possibly someone pointed out the wrong man to you, hmm?'

So rattled was she that she almost fell into that one. Just in time she saw the jaws of the trap. 'I just assumed... I guess I made a mistake...'

'And a very revealing one,' he murmured to her dismay. 'Do I take it, Beth, that you're going to suddenly lose your deliciously intense interest in me now that you've discovered that I'm not my extremely rich and influential—not to mention *married*—elder brother?'

Elizabeth knew when to quit. But that didn't stop her wanting to have the last word.

'I'm not interested in you *or* your brother,' she said frostily, realising with delight that she was now off the hook where Uncle Simon was concerned. Relief made her final line haughtily smug.

'All I'm interested in is the fact that your ridiculous attitude is going to make me late for lunch. And since you've probably damaged a valuable camera by your actions this morning I'll expect to receive an appropriate refund on my bill. I'm sure, seeing as you're the hotel *manager*, it's the least you can do!'

CHAPTER SIX

'I CAN'T possibly stay here!'

The young Melanesian staffer lost his wide, ingratiating smile as he set down Elizabeth's suitcase.

'There is nowhere else. The hotel is full.'

'What about staff quarters?'

Now she had offended him. 'We couldn't put up a *guest* in *staff* accommodation!'

The personal residence of the manager was obviously in a totally different category.

'Not even if the guest requests it?'

A shrug, but one that was stubborn rather than helpless. 'It would not be permitted. The reputation of the hotel——'

'And what about *my* reputation?' Elizabeth interrupted furiously.

'There is much room here. It is very comfortable.' There was no doubt about that. The bungalow was huge and even more blatantly luxurious than any of the guest accommodation she had seen. No, it was not the space, but the *company* she strenuously objected to.

The young man's liquid brown gaze was lowered, but not before Elizabeth had seen the trace of sly amusement. Her eyes burned with violet fire. Her reputation, at least among the staff, had obviously already suffered considerably!

Elizabeth drew a tense, steadying breath. 'Where is he?'

'Who?'

He knew very well who.

'Monsieur Hawkwood.' So much for her vow after their clash yesterday that she was going to avoid him at all costs!

'Oh...' The brown eyes still evaded hers as the young man quickly down-graded his former air of importance. 'I do not know. I am only domestic staff.'

If his skin hadn't been so dark Elizabeth was sure she would have been able to see a blush. If he knew, he certainly wasn't telling.

'Never mind. I'll hunt him to ground myself,' she said grimly, confusing him with her very English metaphor.

'Please, *chérie*, do try and curb your eagerness for me in front of my staff...'

Elizabeth spun around to find her tormentor leaning lazily against the connecting door between the two adjoining suites. He was dressed all in white, a short-sleeved shirt hanging open over his chest and white jeans that were soft with age conforming closely to his hard thighs.

Elizabeth immediately felt hot and overdressed in the dress she had hurriedly pulled on when she had been awoken by a hammering on her roof. She hadn't been able to have her usual morning shower because the water to her bungalow had been switched off. Then Henri had swooped in and started gathering up her possessions, not even giving her time to brush her hair or put on a minimum of make-up before she left.

She lifted her chin and narrowed her eyes accusingly. 'You——'

He neatly cut short her harangue before it started. 'Thank you for doing your job so proficiently, Henri. I'll take care of Miss Lamb from here...'

Elizabeth was barely able to contain herself long enough for Henri's clean bare soles to hit the doorway before she let her frustration fly.

'What am I doing here?'

'As I'm hotel manager it's the least I can do in the unfortunate circumstances,' he purred, cleverly turning yesterday's rash words back on her.

'What circumstances?' demanded Elizabeth suspiciously, pushing a wayward curl off her face. Since she hadn't had a chance to wash and blow-dry her hair into its usual sleekness this morning, it waved around her shoulders in glossy abandon.

'Why, the leak in your roof, of course—and the lack of an alternative place for you to stay.'

'Considering that it hasn't rained since I got here I don't see how anyone could have discovered a leak in my roof,' Elizabeth snorted sarcastically. She didn't consider the fine mist of drops that had briefly swept the beach yesterday afternoon rain.

'Actually, we've had several millilitres,' Jack corrected her with infuriating punctiliousness. 'And—*as I'm manager*—it's my responsibility to make sure that every part of this hotel functions perfectly.'

He was going to throw that phrase back in her face at every opportunity, Elizabeth realised angrily.

'I don't see why I have to move out!'

'You certainly wouldn't be comfortable without power or water and with construction noise going on around you. You see, we have discovered, in the process of investigating your leak, that your bungalow requires some extensive structural alterations to bring it back up to the hotel's exceptionally high standard——'

'Piffle!' They both knew the roof was not the real issue here. The workmen were up there for the express purpose of driving Elizabeth Lamb off his island.

'Bless you,' he murmured solicitously, at his most blandly French. 'I hope you haven't caught a cold by staying in leaky accommodation.'

'How long is it going to take to make these "extensive" alterations?' she asked, already knowing the answer.

'Certainly not less than ten days.'

Quite. The exact length of time she had left at the Isle of Hawks. He *definitely* wanted her off the island.

'What about the people in the other side of my bungalow? Are you kindly putting *them* up here, too?' she demanded.

'Their booking was made prior to yours, so of course they had first option on the only alternative suite that was available,' he said suavely. 'Is there some problem with the arrangement? Our quarters here are quite separate, except for this adjoining door. And you won't be charged for the inconvenience. In fact, to demonstrate the sincerity of the hotel's apologies, *as manager*, I can arrange for the total cost of your holiday to be refunded for you...'

There was no question about it now. He was letting her know that if she left it would be greatly to her financial advantage. Elizabeth was torn by two powerful urges. One was to grab the offer and retreat while she still had a shred of integrity left, the other was to fling his bribe in his mocking face.

'In fact, Beth, you should consider yourself privileged because it's usually only friends of the family who use this suite,' he added, watching her expressive face.

That prompted another unpalatable thought. 'And would I be expected to share my "privileged" accommodation with Mrs Corvell?' She knew that Serena had been using the room, and guessed that the other woman would be no keener than herself at the idea of enforced companionship.

'Serena is no longer staying at Ile des Faucons.'

Elizabeth locked her jaw to prevent it from dropping. 'Oh!'

'She flew back to New Zealand this morning. My brother won't be visiting the island after all.'

'Oh.' Elizabeth's uninterest overwhelmed her momentary surprise. She was just grateful that she was no longer involved in any way with the distasteful triangle . . . or was it a quartet?

'So now you will be able to relax after all, and enjoy the facilities we have to offer for their own sake,' Jack said silkily.

'And if I said I wanted to leave New Caledonia no doubt you'd offer to pay for that, too,' snapped Elizabeth.

'Oh, no, Beth, for you it's not going to be that easy,' he said, to her total consternation.

'What do you mean?' She had been sure he was trying to make her so uncomfortable that she would jump at the first opportunity to leave.

'Well, to leave one requires a passport . . .'

'But I have a——' She didn't, of course. The hotel had it. *He* had it.

He watched the realisation hit her. 'I regret to inform you, Miss Lamb, that owing to an...administrative oversight your passport has been temporarily misplaced. I'm sure it will soon be found, especially if you...co-operate.'

'Co-operate?' The way he pronounced the word made it sound deeply ominous.

His mouth was a hard curve of satisfaction as he studied her utter confusion.

'Yes. You *do* know what co-operation is, don't you, Beth? You give me something *I* want, I give you something you *need*—i.e. your passport?'

'Are—are you trying to *blackmail* me?' Elizabeth's voice was shrill with outrage.

'Ah, you say that as if you've never even heard of such a shocking thing, *chérie*, let alone contemplated doing it yourself——'

'I have *never* blackmailed anyone in my *life*!'

'Oh, very good! Excellent!' He rewarded her with a slow, insulting clap of his hands. 'Such surprise. Such blushing innocence!'

Elizabeth's flush was one of fury, not innocence. 'Are you saying that you won't give me my passport back, even if I offer to leave?'

'And such intelligence, too!' He applauded again.

'Will you stop that?' She swatted wildly at his hands. He raised them in a gesture of surrender, laughing at her frustration. Suddenly the reason for their surroundings became all too clear as she recalled their last encounter.

'If you think I'm going to let you threaten me into your bed——'

The arrested expression on his face told her that she had just made yet another ghastly mistake in judging him. She had allowed her own sensual awareness to invest his words with a completely different meaning from that intended.

'Goodness, Eliza-Beth,' he said wonderingly. 'You *do* have a naughty imagination. And a most disappointing opinion of my manhood. You think I have to *bribe* women into having sex with me?'

'I—no—of course not...' She tried to back-track to no avail. He was right on her heels, enjoying himself enormously.

'Am I so totally unattractive that no woman could find me appealing enough to desire me for myself?'

'Don't be silly,' she muttered quellingly.

'Or is it that you perceive in me a dark, sexual perversity that borders on sadism? Maybe I like to see women cower and cringe...' He had moved even closer, lightly, on the balls of his feet, like a boxer dancing up to an opponent he intended to annihilate with a sucker-punch, the brooding menace of his expression a threat in itself.

And it was all show. Elizabeth didn't know how she knew it—by all rights she should be running away screaming—but she was so certain that he wouldn't hurt her that she tossed her head disdainfully.

'Then you're picking on the wrong woman. You don't scare me. I'm not going to play victim for your macho gratification.'

His eyes glowed with a strange yellow colour, like sun trying to break through summer storm clouds. 'So I don't scare you?'

If her chin tipped any higher she was going to fall over backwards, but she had to do something to counteract his overwhelming physical impact. 'Not a bit!' she defied him.

The sun broke through, but his smile was a twist of irony and his voice disturbingly quiet.

'Then it's purely one-sided. Because, *ma chère*, you scare the hell out of me.'

That did frighten her. She could fight an arrogant man, but a vulnerable one was capable of undermining her defences. Why should she scare him? Wasn't *he* the one with all the money, the power...?

'*Why* are you doing this?' She summoned aggression to mask her uncertainty.

It was as if he scented her secret weakness. Like a hawk's, his strike was swift and lethal. 'Why? Exactly what *I* want to know. Did you intend all along for Jules to realise what you were doing? And what were you going to do with the results of your snooping? Sell it on the open market, or did you have a more personal method of extortion in mind?'

He picked up something from the lacquered coffee-table which formed a right-angled corner between two rattan couches padded with brightly coloured floral fabric. With a flick of his wrist he fanned out a series of photographs—pictures in which he and Serena Corvell featured with monotonous regularity.

'How dare you take my film?' Her cry was more of dismay than outrage.

'I was just checking whether your camera still worked' With a deft movement of his fingers, reminiscent of a card-sharp, he closed the fan while simultaneously flipping another photograph to the front. 'As you can see, it does.'

The photograph was one of Elizabeth, stalking haughtily away from the camera, her beach-shirt floating up around her hips. He must have taken it yesterday, the instant she had turned away from him and her captive camera. Glumly Elizabeth compared the generous breadth of her hips in the shot with the slender memory of Serena's.

'The zoom, too...'

This showed her in profile, skirting a tree. The shirt was breezily plastered against her body. Somehow it managed not only to show the regrettable span of her hips but also the full thrust of her breasts. To her horror she even thought she could see the outline of her nipples, still taut from their encounter with his chest.

She glared at him, trying not to feel fat and frumpy as well as hot and bothered. There was no point in her denying that she had been photographing him. The proof was in his hands. But proof of what, she had no intention of explaining.

'You can't force me to stay,' she said, striving to sound certain.

He looked down at the photograph in his hand, his thick lashes screening his thoughts. 'Can't I?'

The simple question was enough to make her panic. 'I'll complain——'

'Who to? The manager?' He dragged his thumb over the photograph, and she felt the shiver from her heels to the nape of her neck, as if he had actually physically reached out and stroked her. He looked up, capturing her in the midst of her unwilling fascination with his caress of the glossy paper. 'Or the police?' he murmured softly. 'Yes, I'm sure you'd rather tell all to the local police, wouldn't you, *chérie*?'

It was Elizabeth's turn to look down, thinking frantically. He probably had the local police in his pocket. After she had seen Alain St Clair she didn't care what happened to her, but until then she would just have to try and outface him.

'That won't be necessary,' she told him.

'Why not?'

How he loved the word why.

'Because I've decided to take you up on your generous offer.'

'Which one?'

The expectant glint in his eye warned her not to overreact. 'To let me stay here while my bungalow is being repaired.'

'I knew you'd see it my way.' If this hawk had had feathers he would have preened smugly. 'Now, let me show you where everything is.'

'I'll find out for myself, thank you.' Pointedly Elizabeth walked over to the connecting door and waited for him to leave. 'Does this have a key?'

He looked regretful as he delighted in telling her, 'Unfortunately no. Do you sleep-walk?'

'Fortunately no. However, I do know judo,' she lied.

'I'm surprised you didn't try it out on me yesterday,' he said drily, walking slowly over to her.

'I didn't want to hurt you.'

'But you did anyway, judo or not.'

Her eyes fell automatically to his leg, a twinge of re-membered shame leading her to ask, 'Is it still hurting you?'

'You made me a little stiff for a while, but it passed.'

Elizabeth's eyes jerked up to his face as she blushed uncontrollably, furious with herself when his eyes registered puzzlement for a moment before they caught fire with laughter.

'I didn't mean that as a *double entendre*, Beth, al-though honesty forces me to admit it may have been a Freudian slip.' His teasing slipped between the cracks in her composure. 'I thought that of the two of us I was supposed to be the lascivious rake, but you, *ma belle*, make me feel like an innocent, fumbling boy!'

Elizabeth made sure that the door slammed with satisfying force. *Ma belle* indeed! He needn't think flattering her with false compliments was going to blind her to the fact that he was virtually holding her pris-oner. Not that she wanted to escape just yet!

And as for fumbling boy... there had been nothing fumbling about his kiss yesterday, or the way he had touched her. He had seemed like a man very experi-enced in handling a woman's body. Perhaps he had been referring to her wanton over-reaction to him. Perhaps *he* was the one who needed the key to protect himself from unwanted advances!

Perhaps... Elizabeth was beginning to hate the word as much as Jack did!

The first thing that she did, after she had spent an age in the deliciously hot shower washing the man and the problems he created out of her hair, was to call Uncle Simon—having reversed the charges—and ex-plain succinctly that J.J. Hawkwood had changed his plans and Serena Corvell had flown the coop. There was no point in worrying him with the truth of her crass ineptitude in getting caught, she told herself defensively.

Once he knew that he was the one paying for the call, Uncle Simon was correspondingly succinct in his disappointment.

'Oh, well, them's the breaks,' he said philosophically. 'Better luck next time.'

'Next time?' Elizabeth was appalled at the thought.

'We'll get another shot at him.'

'I hope that's the royal "we",' said Elizabeth sourly.

'Now, darlin', don't let one failure get you down. You did good.' Little did *he* know. 'Just relax and enjoy the rest of your stay.'

Fat chance of that! she thought acidly, when Uncle Simon went on to spoil his selfless advice by adding, 'But keep your ears tuned in case you pick up anything useful. If you get a chance, cultivate the brother and see how much he knows——'

'I'm not Mata Hari, Simon!' snapped Elizabeth. She'd rather cultivate a rattlesnake!

'What?'

To her chagrin she realised she'd said it aloud and she rang off hurriedly, before his detective instincts were fully alerted.

She dried her hair and made her second call, to the St Clair estate, which turned out to be as fruitless as all her others had been. With a sigh she unfolded the map of the island that she had obtained from the tours and charters desk in the hotel foyer. It didn't have the estate marked on it—another concession to the old man's obsession for privacy, she guessed—but a few casual enquiries among the staff had already elicited the information she needed and she had drawn several extra pencil lines on her map. The general area to the northwest of the island which she had been told to avoid was her ultimate goal.

She didn't bother to unpack her suitcase. She didn't think it was worth it for the time she was going to be spending here as a reluctant guest.

Wearing a breezy pink blouse, knee-length khaki shorts and sports shoes suitable for a vigorous walk, and having optimistically retrieved the necklace from the hotel bank, Elizabeth set out on her mission.

At first she followed the single, unsealed road that wound around the island's shoreline, little used by traffic since the only vehicles on the island seemed to be the electric buggies used by the hotel to transport guests to the various treks and water activities on the further beaches. She passed several other walkers and a few joggers taking advantage of the morning coolness to ply their virtuous fitness routines.

When she had gone, by her rough calculation from the sketchy map, about two kilometres north, she halted. Sure enough there was a small track plunging off the road towards the interior of the island marked only 'To Summit'. It led, so the hotel tourist guide had told her, to a look-out on the eastern slopes of the low volcanic ridge that divided the island. However, it wasn't the view that Elizabeth was after. A quick glance over her shoulder reassured her that there was only one person in sight, quite a long way behind her, a jogger who appeared to be struggling to maintain a laggardly pace.

Hitching her soft-sided beach bag more securely over her shoulder, Elizabeth stepped on to the track, breathing more easily as she moved out of sight of the road. She walked briskly, suddenly feeling energetic and adventurous.

The track rose quite steeply for the first twenty minutes and Elizabeth was breathing hard by the time she came to the expected fork. She ignored the 'Summit' sign and took the smaller, unmarked, almost overgrown path to the right.

It was slow going. After another twenty minutes of ducking and shoving at stray branches and several times veering off the crushed-shell pathway by mistake, Elizabeth was beginning to worry. She stopped and twisted the top of the bottle of Perrier water that she had tucked in her bag. The water was only slightly chilled, but it fizzled and stung refreshingly on her tongue. She was sweating freely and she took off the pink scarf that she had used as a belt for her shorts and tied it around her head to keep the moisture from running down into her eyes. For a moment she just stood and enjoyed the quiet. She couldn't even hear any birds, only the soft sigh of the breeze in the upper leaves of the trees that towered above the thick shrubs lining the path, the wild sub-tropical lushness which sprang from the volcanic soil a contrast to the carefully landscaped growth on the sandy flatlands below.

She was replacing the half-empty bottle in her bag when she heard a soft rustle of bushes on the path behind her and whirled around, her heart hammering. She knew there were no large animals on the island, let alone predatory ones, but still she was frightened.

He emerged from the overgrowth at a run, almost knocking down the unexpected stationary object in his path.

It was the jogger from the roadway and he came to an abrupt halt as Elizabeth staggered backwards against the press of leaves.

She felt like screaming when she saw who it was.

'Lost again, Beth?' In running-shorts and a singlet, his taut muscles oiled with sweat, and breathing only slightly hard, Jack Hawkwood made her feel soft and weak. In spite of the laggardly gait that had earlier deceived her he was evidently in the peak of condition, his injured leg notwithstanding.

The lie stuck in her throat. 'Uh——'

'Because if you want the look-out you're on the wrong track. The path to the summit is quite a way back. Well marked, too, I would have thought.'

'Oh.' It was her unaccustomed exertion and the elevation that was making her breathless, Elizabeth decided, not his unexpected presence. 'Then where are you going?' Her mind seethed with suspicion.

'Jogging the same route all the time can get boring,' he said smoothly.

He hadn't really answered her question, Elizabeth realised, and yet he had.

'Are you following me?' she demanded bluntly.

'Now, why would I want to do that?' he countered mildly, but there was an amused gleam in his eye that parodied his surprise.

'To annoy me,' she said furiously.

'Do I annoy you?'

'Will you stop answering a question with a question?' she seethed.

'Sorry. Old habit. Interrogation technique.'

'Interrogation?' The very word sent shivers down Elizabeth's spine.

'Mmm. For a while I was part of an army intelligence unit.'

'A spy?' Another shiver.

His half-smile acknowledged her unease. 'Spies don't wear uniforms. I was a career officer in the French military from the time I left school.'

Elizabeth was diverted. 'What happened—did you get invalided out?' She found it hard to believe, considering the feat of endurance he had just demonstrated, chasing her up a hillside.

'No, I just realised I would prefer to be at the top of a chain of command rather than somewhere in the middle, answerable to people I neither liked nor particularly respected. But the longer you stay in the army and the further you move up in military rank, the greater your chance of being "promoted" out of active service into a desk job. I hate sitting at a desk— that's why I didn't go on to university as my family expected. So I resigned my commission to go into business for myself.'

'Managing one of your brother's hotels?' She would hardly have called that being top of a chain of command.

His smile became a grin. 'No. As a security consultant, offering anti-terrorist protection to companies and businessmen dealing with the hot-beds of the Middle East.'

He paused, studying her struggle to look uninterested when in reality curiosity was eating her up.

'That's how I got this,' he added tantalisingly, tapping his scarred thigh. 'An...unforeseen complication during a job in Lebanon.' He paused again, waiting for her response to the enticing lure.

'Unforeseen complication.' Elizabeth repeated his words slowly, unwilling to make it a question. Little did she realise that her violet eyes were brilliant with the interest she stubbornly tried to deny him.

'A woman who turned out to be not what she seemed.'

Elizabeth's resistance crumpled like cardboard. 'And what did she seem to be?'

His mouth thinned to a cynical line. 'A woman in love.'

'With *you*?' So his scarring had been not only physical.

'Do I seem so unlovable?'

'No—I—— No!' She was flustered by the sensual undertone in his question. 'And were you in love with her?'

'At the time very much so.' There was no longer a hint of amusement about him, and Elizabeth found a grave, serious Jack Hawkwood even more threatening to her emotional equilibrium than the cynical rake who had menaced and aroused her. 'Or, at least, in love with the woman I *thought* she was. Zenobia was supposedly working for an international finance group I was liaising with, but she was also an informant for one of the terrorist organisations—some obscure splinter group that was looking to make the headlines. Only I didn't find that out until afterwards—a great intelligence officer I turned out to be!' His self-derision was bleak. 'The information that she passed on enabled them to ambush my car with a rocket attack that killed two of my clients and almost killed me.'

'W-what happened to her?' The grimness in his voice warned her that the woman had not gone unpunished for her betrayal.

'Oh, Zenobia was only a small cog in a fanatical machine and therefore expendable. She was in the car at the time.'

Elizabeth sucked in a breath. 'She was killed?'

'Instantly.' The word was clipped, precise.

'I'm sorry,' she said helplessly.

'For what? My being a gullible fool? For not doing my job properly?'

'*You* didn't cause their deaths——'

'Indirectly I was responsible. I didn't actually hand-feed Zenobia the information——' He looked at her as he clarified with deliberate bluntness, 'I never was one to indulge in pillow talk and ironically I thought Zenobia would be safer in total ignorance of my activities. But evidently she picked up enough to make it worth her while to stay with me. I thought myself in love and lost my edge, not to mention my reputation. Security consultants who lose their clients literally also lose their professional credibility.'

'So...you went into the family hotel business instead.' Had he come to Ile des Faucons to lick his wounds, to hide from what he felt was a humiliating failure? And when he fully recovered would he be back out there again, risking his life in a private war against terrorism? 'How long has it been?' she asked.

She was expecting him to say a year or even less, so she was shocked when he murmured, 'Five years.'

'Five *years*?'

He read her effortlessly. 'Did you think this was just a panacea for my ills?' His eyes silvered with lazy amusement. 'I'm doing exactly what I want to do, Beth. I never coveted my brother's inheritance as eldest son, but this place is rather special...we spent most of our childhood here. As far as I'm concerned I've come home. I also discovered, rather to my surprise, that I happen to be damned good at running a hotel...at the hands-on stuff as opposed to the boring business end that's Jules's forte. Here I'm in command of myself and Ile des Faucons is my sole domain—I virtually have *carte blanche* with the place—Jules's way, I suspect, of consoling me for only being second son...'

'And you don't pine at all for your old life?' Elizabeth asked curiously. Uncle Simon had told her about some of the thrill-junkies he had known from his time in the army—the men who required the constant adrenalin-rush of dicing with death to give them their 'high'. The kind of men who became mercenaries in times of peace in order to satisfy their craving for action. Jack had been a kind of mercenary.

He shrugged. 'I'm a realist. I'm no longer young. I'm fit, but this leg will never be one hundred per cent reliable in the way that it needs to be for the kind of fieldwork I specialised in—which would have meant me doing the kind of desk job I'd left the army to avoid. So I turned the operation over to my partner and came here to convalesce and re-think my life. When I found myself making excuses not to leave I knew I'd found my new niche. These days if I want thrills I can get all I need in the casino, where the only thing I risk losing is money.'

Of which he obviously had plenty. But still Elizabeth didn't believe that he was as settled as he claimed. As much as he denied it his restless edge was still there, and he was subconsciously looking for something to hone it against. That something right now being Elizabeth. It seemed a very unequal challenge!

'Intelligence training is invaluable in running a hotel,' he continued musingly. 'I can generally spot the trouble-makers before they cause trouble and I'll never again make the elementary mistake of being too trusting, no matter how innocent the face...'

So absorbed was Elizabeth in adjusting to what he had just revealed about himself that she didn't notice the words were aimed very specifically at her. 'We all need to trust in something and someone, Jack, it's human nature,' she murmured. 'One betrayal doesn't make the whole world untrustworthy.'

'Are you saying that I can trust *you*, Beth?'

She blinked at the unexpected question and then looked hurriedly away from the piercing grey eyes, flushing uncomfortably.

He folded his arms across his chest. 'I thought not.'

Although his expression was sardonic his words were spoken with a wry amusement that increased as he regarded her unease.

'In that case, Beth, in view of our mutual distrust, I think it would be an advantage on both sides to— *cultivate* a closer understanding of each other...'

It was that tiny hesitation before the word, along with the mocking hint of emphasis, that alerted Elizabeth. She had opened her mouth to accuse him furiously of listening in to her phone calls when she realised that to do so would open herself to all sorts of

awkward questions. She went into a cold sweat just
thinking about it. If he found out what her Uncle
Simon did for a living he would soon ferret out the rest.

He raised his eyebrows as she snapped her mouth
shut, almost biting her tongue.

'You were going to say something?'

'I was yawning,' she denied cuttingly. 'I find this
conversation becoming rather boring...'

'Really? I'm finding it very interesting. In fact I find
all your conversations fascinating, Beth...'

Now she was positive. Either he had listened in personally to the calls she had made from his bungalow or
he had had someone else do it. Perhaps he had even
had them recorded! In the depths of her naïveté
Elizabeth had never even considered the possibility of
such deviousness. She was savagely pleased she had
called him a snake. She glared at him, her mouth
quivering with the frustration of controlling her temper.

'I do look forward to us getting to know each other
better,' he continued in that sultry French accent. 'It'll
be so much easier now that we're living together.'

'We are not living together!' Elizabeth rasped
hoarsely.

'Hmm, that does suggest a personal intimacy we
haven't yet achieved,' he agreed tauntingly.

'Nor ever will!' added Elizabeth emphatically.

'You think not?' He reached out and touched her
trembling mouth with a gentle finger. Elizabeth's lips
parted as if stung. He laughed, a low, slow, sexy rumble that brushed across her skin as he leant closer, his
hand sliding around into her wind-sifted hair so that his
palm possessively cupped the delicate nape of her neck

while his fingers interwove with the sun-warmed strands. 'Poor little lamb, your thinking is as woolly and disordered as this soft pelt of yours. That's the trouble with lying, *chérie*; it gets you all confused, mixes up dreams and reality until you don't really know where you are...'

Elizabeth knew exactly where she was and why she shouldn't be there. The ripping talons of a hunting hawk were not supposed to feel so achingly wonderful to its prey. His second hand joined the first and she struggled against the startling discovery of how sensual a scalp massage could be as his hard fingers dug and kneaded at the sensitive flesh while his mouth glided closer and closer...

The voluptuous tingling spread from her scalp to the rest of her body, further weakening her feeble resistance. She was going to bite him if he dared kiss her mouth, Elizabeth told herself dizzily, but he didn't give her the chance to satisfy her hunger. His mouth disappointingly bypassed hers, the hands in her hair tightening to pull her head back so that he could nuzzle at her throat, the warm, moist caress finally settling against the hot pulse just under her left jaw. His tongue was wet and rough as it sanded the betraying leap of blood in her veins. She gasped, clutching his waist as he sucked gently and then bent her head the other way so that he could pay equal homage to the opposite pulse.

Only then when he had tasted her thoroughly did he seek out her mouth, murmuring thickly with satisfaction as she carried out her mental threat and sank her white teeth sighingly into the satiny curve of his lower lip. The masculine flavour of him exploded through her

senses and Elizabeth didn't realise how rough and uncontrolled she had become until she tasted the salt in
her mouth and realised what she had done. She
moaned and wrenched her head away, looking in horror at the red pearl beading on his lip.

He licked at it, revealing the small split to her mor-
tified gaze. 'First blood to you, *chérie.*'

The cool grey eyes flared brilliantly, sending her a
smouldering message of savage approval that totally
eluded her as she stared, aghast, at what she had done,
not in defensive anger as she had planned, but in excessive eagerness.

'I—I'm sorry,' she said, her voice stifled with mor-
tification.

He let her back nervously out of his relaxed grasp,
although his body was tensely alert as he watched her
curious reaction to the evidence of her spontaneous
passion.

'I'm not, I liked you biting me,' he said in a dark
tone that was as soft and rasping against her nerves as
his tongue had been against her skin. '"Rich the
treasure, Sweet the pleasure; Sweet is pleasure after
pain."'

She was too upset by her loss of control to be im-
pressed by his knowledge of seventeenth-century
English poetry, or to fully comprehend his meaning.
She stared at him in confusion, prompting him to utter the statement of silky warning that had her scuttling down the hillside in ignominious retreat.

'I don't know precisely what it is you're up to on my
island, Beth, but you may as well know now that I fully
intend to find out. It would save us both a lot of time
and grief if you just confessed here and now, while I'm

in a relatively mellow mood. It might help you make up your mind to know that I still have close contacts in my former business, and that sooner or later I'm going to know everything there is to know about you.

'It's your choice, *chérie*: with me or against me.'

CHAPTER SEVEN

ELIZABETH looked with dismay at the huge pile of gambling chips on the table in front of her. The croupier was pushing yet another stack towards her and she could feel the other gamblers pressing in, waiting with feverish tension for her to place her next bet so they could follow suit and share the extraordinary luck that seemed to dog her whenever she set foot in the hotel casino.

She knew next to nothing about gambling and had only chosen roulette because there didn't appear to be any concentration or skill involved, nothing to distract her from her covert surveillance of Jack and Serena. Tonight she had been even more distracted, her whole being committed to a course of action that was totally against every principle she possessed.

'*Mesdames et monsieurs*, place your bets, please...'

Recklessly Elizabeth pushed all the chips in front of her on to the layout. If she could lose everything perhaps all these people would lose interest and stop staring at her. The last thing she wanted was an audience for the performance to come. She wasn't playing with her own money anyway, since all her chips were the legitimate offspring of the complimentary five-thousand franc casino voucher provided in each guest's room.

'I want it all on number one,' she told the man standing impassively at the end of the table, moistening her dry throat with the martini that sat at her elbow.

A concerted gasp spread around the table, followed by a flurry of whispers.

'You wish to place all your chips on a straight bet?' The croupier was well trained, his face expressionless. 'Do you wish this bet to be in addition to your existing standing bets?'

Elizabeth's violet eyes glittered with a feverishness which had nothing to do with gambling. She picked the olive out of her drink and nibbled it, to disguise the fact that she didn't know what a standing bet was, let alone that she had one.

She shook her head. 'I want everything to go on number one,' she said firmly.

'You've got guts, I'll give you that, little lady,' murmured the pudgy, sweating man on her left admiringly. He was an American who had watched her erratic betting at first with condescending amusement and then with envy as she had totally demolished the house odds. 'I'd love to know what your system is.'

So would Elizabeth.

She took another slug of her martini, her eyes sweeping the room as the croupier had a whispered conversation with a white-jacketed colleague whom he had summoned with a glance.

Where in hell was he?

Normally Jack was doing the rounds of the casino at this time, but tonight of all nights he seemed to be nowhere in evidence.

'Another martini, *mademoiselle*?'

A waiter appeared like magic at her elbow, a drink already poised on his tray. Elizabeth took it and absently dropped a handful of chips in its place. The waiter's eyes widened, and he was practically bowing as he backed away.

With a jolt in her chest Elizabeth finally spotted him. He was at the twin-columned entrance to the casino, his dark head bowed as he listened frowningly to the urgent conversation of one of his employees.

Her tension tightened another notch. After several days of fruitlessly trying to escape the attention of him and his league of minions she was once again turning the tables and stalking him. The knowledge of what she was going to do when she caught him made her palms sweat.

She tried to whip up the anger that was essential to her bravado. He deserved everything he got for his actions this past week.

True to his word, he had made her very conscious of the fact that she was at the mercy of the absolute dictatorship on Ile de Faucons. He'd had her watched so closely that she was swamped by over-zealous service wherever she went. Although the door between their adjoining suites had, against all her suspicions, remained firmly closed he still somehow managed to seep into every crack and crevice of her awareness.

In fact his invasion of her privacy was so absolute that he had even begun to invade her dreams and almost seemed to know her plans before she did.

In desperation she had been forced to join group tours pony-trekking, or picnicking or cruising around the island, but Jack had merely pulled rank and tagged along, effortlessly under-cutting the protection a group provided by making sure everyone knew that Elizabeth was the real focus of his devoted attention. Once that was established Elizabeth had found her hastily acquired new acquaintances all too eager to curry favour with the management by playing Cupid. And the appalling truth was that if she hadn't known that he was doing it for the express purpose of harassing and humiliating her Elizabeth might well have found him irresistible!

He was charming and worldly, amusing and intelligent and he was so...all right, he was so *sexy*. Touching her only with his look and his smile, he managed to make her feel a treacherous thrill of desire that disturbed her by its potency. While she could fend off any attack on her intelligence with confidence her senses were not so easy to subdue.

Normally when she was anxious or nervous Elizabeth was quiet, but around Jack that wasn't even an option. He would just needle at her until she responded out of sheer fury, and once she was talking his provocative replies made it impossible to curb her desire to have the last word. She rarely succeeded.

This morning Elizabeth had thought that she had finally managed to outwit the master of cunning. The previous evening she had loudly booked herself on today's shopping and sightseeing tour of the mainland. Then, while Jack was off on his early morning jog, she had sneaked out along the beach to the pier where the hydrofoil which took the weekly all-day trip to the Phare Amedée was moored. The Amedée lighthouse was at the entrance to the encircling reef and Elizabeth had wanted to visit it anyway before she left New Caledonia ... or was deported in handcuffs!

Elizabeth had persuaded the young crewman who was the only person on board so early in the morning to let her go straight on to the boat instead of waiting for the duly appointed boarding time, flagrantly misusing Jack's name to convince him that it didn't matter that her name wasn't on the booking list.

It was only when they were safely twenty minutes out to sea that she allowed herself to go up to the roof-top observation deck and breathe the sweet salt-air of freedom. She had done it! Eight hours from now she would have to return to face Jack's displeasure at being outmanoeuvred, but for the interim she would endeavour to relax and forget about the entire wretched St Clair problem.

Her mind blissfully emptied, she gazed out towards a blurred column of light which was fading in where sea and sky imperceptibly blended. She had put on her straw hat but still had to put a shading hand up to the brim as she squinted across the shining waters.

It wasn't the beacon, but the lighthouse itself shining, proclaiming its dominance over the sea, Elizabeth realised as they neared their destination. The tall, graceful white column perched on the small coral cay was reflecting the rays of the sun to dazzling effect.

The cay itself was tiny, an irregular circle of white beach enclosing a few small buildings among a twist of trees and low shrubs and the lighthouse itself. Their tour party had exclusive visiting rights for the day so the sense of relaxation and isolation was complete and Elizabeth revelled in the pleasure of being an ordinary, unencumbered tourist.

It only took ten minutes to make a circuit of the completely flat island, after which Elizabeth decided that she would try the water while most of the others were investigating the tiny souvenir stall or climbing the lighthouse.

She couldn't help feeling exposed as she left the small changing-shed clutching her towel around her. She had been in so much of a rush when she had fled the hotel that she had forgotten to pack her beach-shirt. Fortunately there were only a few children and elderly couples already settled on the pristine white beach so she didn't feel as self-conscious as usual as she shed the towel and plunged joyously into the water. Its silky warmth and buoyancy were delightful, and by the time she walked back up the beach most of the rest of the party were spreading themselves out along the shore-line.

There were the usual male double-takes at the voluptuousness of her pale-skinned figure in the wet suit, but this time she forced herself to ignore them. She wasn't going to allow a few leering idiots to spoil her precious day of freedom. In fact, she had been a fool to deny herself the pleasure of frequent swimming and sunbathing at the hotel just because she wasn't as slim and tanned as most of the other female guests under forty seemed to be. Judging from the wealth of their clothes and jewellery, they probably didn't have to work for a living and could afford the time and money to pamper themselves into the right shape.

Her determination not to let her acute self-consciousness get the better of her led Elizabeth to stretch out on her towel to dry off, curtly fending off an eager offer to fetch a sun-lounger from one persist-ent drooler. When she felt she had asserted herself enough for one morning she pulled her roomy thigh-length T-shirt over her dry suit and headed for the lighthouse.

Standing on the bare floorboards and looking up the centre well of the iron staircase which curved around the inner walls, she almost lost her nerve but, having paid her fifty francs, Elizabeth's thrifty nature bolstered her wavering pride.

She made sure as she climbed that she kept very close to the wall, her grip on the handrail white-knuckle tight. She had to rest several times before she finally panted out on to the narrow open-air platform that circled the crown of the lighthouse.

She was glad she had waited until last to explore the view. It was like being alone at the top of the world, lord of all she surveyed, three hundred and sixty degrees of cobalt sea and sky, flat, featureless and almost indistinguishable from one another except where the rim of white surf outlined the curve of the reef. The view to the beach below was nauseatingly quick to make her feel dizzy. Elizabeth stepped back against the rough-cast wall, closing her eyes and breathing deeply before she dared open them again.

The thrill became a throat-tightening sensation of doom as her eyes cautiously lowered from sky—to sea—to pier...where a second boat was tying up alongside the hotel transport. A boat which was appallingly familiar.

And there was the pirate himself, dressed in his favoured white, striding off the pier on to the sand, lifting a hand in greeting to the cries of welcome from the small band of caterers and entertainers who had mingled with the guests to travel to the island.

Elizabeth watched, hypnotised, as the black head tilted and he looked up, almost as if he knew exactly where she was. He *couldn't* identify her hat-shaded head, surely, not from *that* distance. She tried to convince herself of it, but as soon as he began to move towards the lighthouse she decided she would not, *could* not, just stay up here waiting. If she had to meet her fate it would be with solid ground under her feet!

Twenty steps back down the iron stairs she knew she was in deep trouble. Going up had been strenuous and nerve-racking, but going down was terrifying. There was nothing in front of her but the sheer fall of steps spinning around the open central shaft. The metal railing suddenly felt horrifyingly insubstantial in her sweaty grip. She froze, both hands gripping the rail, visualising herself free-falling forwards down the hundreds of lethal iron rungs. Her knees trembled and her sandy toes curled inside her canvas shoes. She teetered on the brink of black panic.

'Eliza-Beth?'

The deep voice curled up through the cavernously dim centre of the lighthouse, reverberating through her frozen horror.

'Eliza-Beth? Are you coming down or do I have to come up and get you?'

The idea was such sheer bliss that tears rushed to her eyes. Her first try was such a pitiful croak that her second over-compensated into a harsh scream that sounded graphically like a taunt rather than a desperate plea, 'Come and get me.'

A very explicit string of French swear-words rose like music to her ringing ears then there was the distant sound of steps striking metal, hard, rapid, angry steps, accompanied by a litany of threats that she only hoped she would live long enough for him to carry out!

She kept her eyes resolutely shut for what seemed an age, the echo of his magnifying footsteps confusing her senses until she wasn't sure whether he was coming or going. Suddenly they stopped altogether. Visions of his body floating through the air to smash on the boards far below peeled back her lids.

'Jack? Jean-Jacques?'

He stood on the curve of the staircase just below her, breathing deeply yet silently, a faint sheen of sweat coating his darkly flushed face.

'I'm here, Eliza-Beth.'

He remained motionless and she swallowed at the murder in the stormy grey eyes.

'And I am not happy,' he added redundantly in that calm, threatening voice. He held out his hand, palm up. 'Come. You have made your pointless gesture of defiance and forced me to fetch you. I have ascended to your level, now you will descend to mine.'

If only she could. But her feet were glued to the shallow metal tread. 'I——'

'Don't argue with me, *chérie*.' He interrupted her feeble attempt to overcome her speechless horror with dangerous softness. 'I am in no mood to be trifled with. Be thankful I have chosen not to send you down by the scenic route.'

Elizabeth's uncontrolled shudder nearly overbalanced her. She clutched the railing even more fiercely, her face blanching, and the fury that smoked his eyes flared suddenly into a blazing awareness.

'Beth?'

She looked at him dumbly.

He leapt up the three steps that separated them in one bound and she shrieked in combined fear and rage at his recklessness, abandoning the rail for the more substantial bulk of his body, her clutching hands making him curse as he swayed, gripping the opposite rail with one hand while his other snapped around her waist.

'For God's sake, *chérie*, are you trying to kill us both?'

Her face went milk-white as she buried it in his chest, knocking her hat off her head. He made a grab at it as it whispered beyond his reach, drifted down into the dimness of the centre shaft. 'Don't,' she gasped. 'Don't move.'

'How can I, with you practically crawling inside me? Calm down, *chérie*, I'm not going to let you go——'

'Yes, you are——'

His cheek turned to rub against her soft hair. 'No, I'm not. Why did you come up here if you suffer from vertigo?'

'I don't!' Her voice rose raggedly to deny the accusation of stupidity. 'Heights have never worried me before.'

'But then perhaps you've never been this high before on such a flimsy open staircase.'

Elizabeth moaned into his chest, hopeless tears dampening the white cotton pocket over his steady-beating heart.

'I didn't mean that kind of flimsy,' he said patiently. 'This lighthouse has stood the test of time. It is only dangerous if you are careless, and I am not a careless man.'

'You ran up... your leg... you could have slipped!' she accused shrilly. She refused to take her face out of its warm, comfortable human nest of security.

'You are filled with fear and yet you still find room to be frightened for me?' he said gently. 'I know my capabilities, Beth, and I do have a very good head for heights.' He moved testingly.

'No!' Elizabeth locked her limbs instantly.

'Yes,' he said firmly. 'I can't carry you, Beth—if it were flat ground I could but my leg won't take the strain of all these steps with your added weight. You'll have to do it yourself——'

'I can't!'

'Yes, you can. You're intelligent, you're young and healthy and sternly independent—all excellent qualifications for going up and down staircases.'

'I'll fall.' She hated herself for being so weak but she couldn't help her unreasoning fear.

He tipped her chin up with a firm hand, his stern gaze unrelenting as he studied her tear-washed cheeks. 'No, you won't. Because I'll be in with you, holding your hand with each and every brave step.'

'There's not room for two of us,' she protested.

'Not side by side, no. So I'll be on the step below you.'

'Going down *backwards*?' Elizabeth was awe-stricken with fresh horror. 'No, I won't let you——'

'You'd rather do it entirely by yourself?'

'*No!*'

'Well, then...'

'Please, don't make me do this...' she begged in a shaky whisper.

'I won't have to. You'll make yourself do it. Come on, *chérie*. Before someone else decides to come up...'

Pride warred with her fear. The thought of her pitiful exhibition of abject cowardice being witnessed by anyone else was almost enough to galvanise her frozen limbs—almost...

'Jack...'

He kissed her tear-salty lips. Kissed her with a hard, practised thoroughness until he felt her shock turn to angry confusion, then the tentative beginnings of response.

'Trust me...'

He kissed her again before she could react to his order, holding her very tightly, controlling both her response and his with an aggression that eased only when he raised his head.

'I won't let anything happen to you...' It was a statement of fact rather than a promise as he lowered his head again, smothering her doubts with relentless sensuality that heated her to the tips of her cold extremities.

With each kiss Elizabeth felt the hard knot in her stomach unravel a little further. It was an exercise in male dominance but also a demonstration of strength and certainty that she couldn't help but feel grateful for. When he released her mouth for the last time she took an unsteady breath.

'All right, I'm ready...'

His eyes silvered with mockery. 'So am I, but we'd have to be acrobats to do anything about it here. Wait until I get you on top of me in bed, *chérie*, then I'll show you what *real* vertigo is!'

'My God, you're an arrogant animal,' she said, flushing with a combination of shock and embarrassment, not even noticing as he stepped down in front of her, holding both of her hands in one of his as the other firmly gripped the central rail.

'Thank you.' He held her angry eyes with the hypnotic power of his as he stepped down and drew her down the first step. Before the knowledge of what she had just done registered he murmured, 'Ever thought of entering a wet T-shirt contest? You have such a superb natural advantage, your victory would be a walkover.'

His chin was level with her breasts so that she couldn't mistake the taunt. Embarrassment rapidly turned to rage. She glared at him as she advanced another two steps, searching for some equally insulting retort.

'Ever thought of having a haircut? I hear that the hotel salon does wonderful things with feminine tresses like yours.'

He was undismayed by the slur on his masculinity, probably because they both recognised its absurdity.

'I thought you liked playing with my hair, *chérie*. It certainly gave you something to hold on to that day you were panting in my arms...'

Her eyes were violently purple as they locked with his, her hands tense in his solid grasp as they reached the first landing in the downward spiral.

'I was not *panting*——'

'Moaning, then.'

They argued fiercely on the long, slow journey, she spitting fury even as she realised the deliberate purpose of his outrageous comments. He was doing an extremely good job of keeping her mind on what they were saying and off what they were doing, but he needn't expect her to thank him for his methods!

Reaching the ground was a relief in more ways than one. She had realised during the second half of the descent that she had just given him a perfect opportunity to ruthlessly interrogate her and he hadn't taken it. And if it had occurred to her then it would certainly have occurred to him.

She stared at him as he turned and took her fallen hat from the concerned lighthouse-keeper, reassuring him with a few low words. Why, if he was so suspicious of her, hadn't he grabbed at the chance to use her fear against her?

When he turned back and saw the puzzlement in her eyes his understanding was astonishingly swift and comprehensive. The wry amusement with which he had turned away the lighthouse-keeper's concern hardened into a sardonic bitterness.

'You do not have much of an opinion of my character, do you, *chérie*? I am not so lost to principle that I believe the end always justifies the means. I was supposed to be one of the good guys out there in the big, wide, wicked world, remember?'

She thought of his dead lover, who had not had his scruples, and the price he had paid for her lack, and felt guilty for doubting him.

'I—I don't know how to thank you,' she said awkwardly, trying to make amends with her meekness. She still felt weak and wobbly, and was glad of the hand under her elbow as they stepped back out into the sunshine. 'I don't know what I would have done if you hadn't come along...' Her stilted primness made it sound as if he had just been wandering by, rather than intently pursuing her, and his sardonic expression melted into a punishing grin.

'Just shows you the dangers of sneaking off on your own,' he murmured silkily, placing her hat back on her glossy head. 'And the necessity of accepting help when it's offered, instead of stubbornly trying to do everything by yourself. Don't worry about thanking me, Beth; I'm sure I'll eventually think of some suitable way in which you can express your gratitude.'

She looked at him warily, half expecting him to start bombarding her with belated questions, but again he confounded her by escorting her back to her things on the beach, setting up one of the gaily striped umbrellas over her towel and fetching her a drink bristling with fruit and flowers, while he chatted inconsequentially about the history of the lighthouse and the marine life of the surrounding reef.

'What's in this?' Elizabeth asked, as she took the chilled glass he handed her, eyeing its pink-tinged contents doubtfully.

'Knock-out drops,' he said cheerfully. 'I thought I'd render you unconscious, smuggle you aboard my yacht and sail off into the wide blue yonder so that I could ravish you at leisure.'

Elizabeth took a hurried gulp of the mildly alcoholic cocktail, terrified at how appealing his words sounded, and started to cough.

'Was that an act of faith, or eagerness, *chérie*?' He knelt on the sand beside her, his tall glass of beer tilting precariously as he slapped her back with what she thought unnecessary force. Then, ignoring her spluttering, he rummaged in a white canvas bag that had appeared among her things and produced a bottle of sunblock lotion.

'Remove your clothes and lie down.'

Elizabeth wondered if the drink had gone straight to her head, or perhaps his faultless English had failed him for once.

'I beg your pardon?'

'I choose not to grant it . . . *yet*. Even under the umbrella you will burn if you don't use cream. Your skin is so fine and pale.'

'I'll keep my T-shirt on——'

'Later, then, when we swim.'

Her vision went hazy at the thought of his hands massaging lotion into her sun-warmed flesh. She would certainly need the cool embrace of the water afterwards!

'I—I've already had my swim . . .' Mesmerised, she watched him wedge his beer into the sand and unselfconsciously shed his own clothes to reveal the familiar blue swimming-trunks.

'And snorkelled over the reef?' He uncapped the lotion, poured it into his cupped hand and stroked it across his chest and belly.

'No, I——'

'You can come with me.'

As she watched his hands move over his body an indecent interpretation of his words popped into her mind. *Oh, yes* . . .

Swiftly she clamped down on the renegade thought. 'I've never dived before . . .'

'And you don't handle first times very well—yes, I remember you telling me,' he said, not seeming to notice her absorption with his actions. Dry-mouthed, she waited for him to ask her to do his back, knowing she couldn't refuse without sounding ridiculously prudish.

To her chagrin he didn't ask. He very deftly applied all the lotion himself, with a few minor contortions that had the effect of showing off some very impressive musculature. She couldn't help her gaze drifting down to the scarred thigh almost touching hers.

'Do you want me to cover it up?' he asked.

Her eyes flashed to his face. Hers, still a little pale from her ordeal, pinkened under the shady brim of her hat as she saw that he, too, was recalling her instinctive response to his previous mention of his 'deformity'.

'No, of course not,' she said.

'You like my body?' He stretched out beside her, tucking his arms behind his head.

With difficulty she held his gaze coolly. 'What's not to like?' she murmured with a sophistication that she hoped matched his.

His smile was sultry. 'Damned with faint praise, hmm, Beth? Yours is magnificent. I don't know why you hide it as if you are embarrassed to possess it.'

'I'm not embarrassed.'

'Shy, then.'

He made her sound silly and immature. 'I'm not shy, I just dislike being ogled simply because I'm...I'm...'

'Beautiful.'

'Big,' she corrected him flatly.

'Big?' he echoed, as if he didn't understand the word.

'Too big,' she clarified, flushed and furious with him for cornering her into saying it.

Instead of mocking her, or making the suggestive remark she expected, he looked gravely into her defiant eyes.

'Of course you are too big—for a boy or a prepubescent girl. But why should you deny your femininity by forcing yourself into a strait-jacket of unnatural body shape? Your curves may be "unfashionable" in the model-girl sense but in the real world they are the quintessence of womanliness.

'As for "ogling", how else can we men express admiration for a woman except by looking? When I look at you I'm vividly aware of myself as male, and the fantasy that you might similarly enjoy looking at *me* is a deeply satisfying one...'

'Funny, I hadn't tagged you for a feminist,' Elizabeth quipped weakly, suffused with glowing warmth at his sincerity.

His shrug was very French. 'I like women. I don't like labels; they are so confining. Yours, I think, you have clung to as a form of defence mechanism.'

'Against what?' she dared challenge him.

'Against men. Against yourself...'

The challenge instantly lost its savour. 'You talk in riddles.'

'You *are* a riddle.'

Her chin lifted. 'Not one *you're* going to solve.'

'I'm well on the way already. I have learned some very interesting things about you from my well informed sources. You have never been married or engaged. You work for a happily married middle-aged professor in whom you have no romantic interest, and have an excellent reputation with the university. You also administrate your uncles' bookshop. You don't seem to have time for any hobbies...except reading, therefore your life, although filled with people, is also oddly solitary. How am I doing so far, Lady Mystery?'

Far too well. Elizabeth instinctively sought to deny the dangerous rush of adrenalin through her veins at his challenge, and decided on defiant distraction, pulling off her T-shirt and leaning back on her hands as a symbolic gesture of contempt for the suggestion that she had anything to hide.

He watched lazily as she applied the coconut-scented cream to her exposed skin, making her feel as if she was putting on an exhibition purely for his benefit—which she was, she admitted ruefully to herself, conscious of the forbidden pleasure of touching herself under his gaze.

Elizabeth allowed her fingers to linger caressingly over their task and instead of sunning herself in a pose that minimised her generous proportions she arched out contentedly, like a cat in the sun, and when she swam she didn't come out as she had previously, with arms crossed protectively under her chest, but strolled up the beach with her hands swinging naturally at her sides and stood and patted herself dry with a brazen insouciance that made Jack groan and roll over on his stomach in a gesture more explicit than words.

Elizabeth knew that she was flirting with disaster by letting her guard down, but the shock in the lighthouse, followed by the woozy alcoholic counter-punch of the floral cocktail and the sensuously enervating effect of the blazing sun, warm sand and silky sea combined to invest the remainder of the day with a magic unreality that she gratefully accepted. Time slipped out of joint, aided by a very lazy, undemanding Jack

Hawkwood who seemed as content as she to maintain a tacit truce.

He showed her how to snorkel and rescued her when she dived down to where the fish schooled so thickly that she got frighteningly lost in their abundance. He sat with her during the updated Amedée version of the traditional Melanesian 'bougna'—a feast of fish with taro and yams bathed in coconut milk and wrapped in banana leaves to cook on hot stones—and laughingly urged her on when she and some of the other guests were dragged up to perform in the equally traditional dance and song demonstration which followed.

Later, they drank coffee on the beach and watched while one of the attractive young dancers showed the many ways in which a pareau could be worn over a swimsuit, and Jack had insisted on buying one for her, teasing her when it fell off at her first attempt at tying it and coming to her aid with a deftness that made her fleetingly jealous.

By the end of the day, mellowed even further by a slight overdose of sun, Elizabeth didn't turn a hair at the suggestion that she sail back with Jack rather than travel with the rest on the hydrofoil. She wanted to wring the last drop of pleasure from their unspoken truce.

A breeze had sprung up and with it a choppy sea, and the ride home was an exhilarating one, Elizabeth content, silently enjoying the sight of Jack exercising his mastery over the elements, his powerful legs braced against the deck, his shirtless torso glistening with spray as his muscles rippled at each pull and tug of the wheel.

The voyage ended all too soon, accompanied by an unpleasant shock that sobered Elizabeth suddenly and completely.

As he was handing her from the boat to the pier in front of the hotel, Jack casually let slip that he was lunching with his grandfather the next afternoon.

'Your grandfather?' Elizabeth's curiosity had mingled with a leap of hope that was strangely sour. His absence might give her the chance to make another assault on the fortress of St Clair! 'Does he live on the mainland?'

'My mother's father—and no, he lives right here on the Ile des Faucons. He's not in the best of health and I take my duty to him very seriously.'

'Is your grandmother still alive?' Jack had already mentioned that his widowed mother had remarried some years before and was now living with her new family in Switzerland.

Jack crouched to check the knot on the mooring line. 'No, she was killed during the war and *Grandpère* was badly wounded. The family estate was literally devastated by fighting and most of their personal possessions were looted or destroyed. Fortunately the family's bankers were Swiss, so when *Grandpère* decided to abandon Europe along with his bad memories he had sufficient wealth to indulge his whim to recreate the beauty that the Germans had ransacked and destroyed.' He rose to his feet and turned to face Elizabeth, who was suddenly experiencing an awful presentiment of disaster.

'So actually the St Clair estate here is an almost perfect replica of the St Clair château near Lille as it was in its heyday—even down to its furnishings,' he finished.

Elizabeth couldn't remember now what she had said to get away, but she hoped the reeling shock that had numbed her mind had also numbed her expression.

Jack Hawkwood could get her into the St Clair estate.

The thought had grown from a tiny fearful seed into a full-blown determination. If Alain St Clair was too ill to invite her into his well guarded citadel then Jack must be her invitation card.

'I take my duty to him very seriously.' In other words Jack would probably take an extremely dim view of any perceived attempt to swindle a sick old man. What would his reaction be if he discovered that Elizabeth was carting around a chunk of his family's precious and—thanks to the Nazis—extremely rare personal heritage?

Somehow she didn't think that it would be pleasant. He was already predisposed to distrust Elizabeth, and she couldn't blame him. She needed time to smooth things over with his grandfather. If she could get *him* on her side then Jack would have to respect his wishes...and if she used *Jack* to get to his grandfather the old man might be more inclined to listen to a friend of his grandson's than the niece of two virtual strangers. There was a chance yet that the untidy ends of this unfortunate affair could all be wrapped up very quickly and neatly—providing she could think of a way to get Jack's unknowing co-operation...

'I understand you want to challenge the house?'

Elizabeth nearly jumped out of her seat when the question purred in her ear. The sights and sounds of the casino faded in again, along with a shuddering awareness of the man standing just behind her, the hand he had placed on the velvet padding of her chair touching her back. Her bare back. The little black dress that she had hurriedly bought from the hotel's exclusive fashion boutique late this afternoon was as revealing as it was expensive—scooping almost to the dimples in the base of her spine at the back and deeply square across her breasts in front, baring more of their fullness than had her modest swimsuit.

She tilted her head to look at him, at an angle that she knew would give him a splendid view of her cleavage. 'What *is* the house limit?'

His eyes ignored the unsubtle invitation, his smile a thin slash in a face that was coolly unreadable as he looked at the untidy heap of chips in front of her.

'For you? The sky.' He nodded curtly to the croupier and the wheel began to spin. 'I hope you're feeling lucky tonight, Beth.'

She made herself laugh softly at the hint of threat. 'Why? You're the one who could lose his shirt.'

She flicked a provocative finger at the pearl buttons on his white shirt, slightly amazed at her temerity. In black trousers and tie and a white jacket he almost looked like the archetypal conservative sophisticate until you noticed the reckless counterpoint of the sleeked-back hair and flash of gold in his ear.

'I'm not playing and the house is well cushioned against the whims of high-rollers,' he murmured, the merest glint in his eyes suggesting that he wasn't as cool as he seemed to be. 'Do you know how much you're staking here?'

'No more than I can afford to lose,' she said airily, unwilling to admit she didn't and annoyed that his eyes still hadn't wandered to her blatantly wicked dress. Was he blind? Why was it when you *wanted* a man to ogle you he wouldn't? She picked up her fresh martini and defiantly tossed it off with one gulp.

'How many of those have you had?' He sounded vaguely disapproving. He who had practically *plied* her with drinks that very afternoon. Hypocrite!

'Dozens!' she lied, smiling at him brilliantly. Damn it, she *would* get a response from him. She half turned in her seat, draping her elbow over his hand on the chair-back so he could see how the clever slit in her square bodice parted tantalisingly with the movement. 'Your staff obviously know how to take care of a winner!'

While everyone else's attention had been riveted on the dance and bounce of the ball over the red and black pockets, Jack was grimly amused to notice that his novice high-roller didn't seem to give a damn what was happening on the table. Whatever game she was playing, it obviously wasn't motivated by avarice.

'I, on the other hand, am an expert at consoling the losers,' he said suavely, 'which you must admit is by far a more challenging task. I look forward to your comments on my technique.'

She glared suspiciously at the hand he held out.

'Why should I?'

'Because, *ma chère*, I'm afraid your luck just changed infinitely for the worse. You just lost your entire thirty thousand francs.'

CHAPTER EIGHT

NEARLY nine thousand New Zealand dollars!

Elizabeth glared over at the man dealing with the gold-foiled top of a champagne bottle in the small but luxuriously equipped kitchen. It wasn't the first time Jack had invited her into his suite of rooms, but it was the first time she had been reckless enough to accept. Normally she would have been gazing around intently, curious to see how he lived, but at the moment she couldn't care less.

If she had known what her chips had been worth she *never* would have thrown them away with that last, stupid bet. Why, with that much money she might have been able to *bribe* somebody into forgetting their loyalty to Hawk Hotels long enough to help her. As it was she was left with Plan A which, having got her this far, was rapidly losing its angry momentum.

'You might find it a little breezy outside on the veranda at this time of night, so why don't we just sit in here with the french doors open ... ?'

Elizabeth took the glass that Jack handed her and inhaled the heady burst of bubbles as she followed him over to the deep-cushioned white leather couch that faced the dark, quiet bay. Although the casino and hotel disco were still open there was no sight or sound of activity at this end of the grounds. They might as well be alone together on a desert island, Elizabeth thought nervously as she sank into the thick cushions. She expected Jack to sit down beside her but instead he chose the far end of the couch, his body angled towards her. He had shed his jacket and the black tie dangled freely from one point of his loosened collar, his white shirt unbuttoned just enough that she could see the beginnings of the dark pelt of hair that covered his chest.

The light from the standard lamp behind him threw half his face into shadow and the half that she could see clearly was darkly saturnine, and her misgivings increased. He had seemed perfectly receptive a few minutes ago when she had accepted his offer of a champagne consolation prize for her spectacular losses. When she had realised that he intended her to have it at the casino bar she had pinned on her best pout and suggested somewhere a little more private.

A brief spark of fire had glowed in the silver eyes. 'How private is a little more?' he had murmured, his hand firm on her waist as he guided her away from the roulette table, his thigh brushing hers as they navigated the crowd.

'I...there's something I need to talk to you about...' She thought the little stammer was a nice touch, and through her long, dark lashes she gave him the kind of glance calculated to fan that silver glow into a smoulder. 'It's rather...awkward and I'd prefer to keep it just between the two of us.'

The hand on her waist, by accident or design, slipped from her hip to rest on the bare skin at the base of her spine, and Elizabeth nearly went through the roof at the warm friction of his palm.

'Would my office do?'

Of course he would have one, even though he didn't seem to spend any time there. The hotel he managed ran so smoothly that there was bound to be mountains of behind-the-scenes work, particularly for someone like Jack whose lazy public persona existed in tandem with a private man whose former profession had trained mind and body to be extremely exacting and disciplined in everything he did.

'Well...' She balked at the idea of trying to seduce Jack's unwitting assistance in an environment where he was used to being on his mettle. She needed him relaxed and completely off-guard. 'It's very *personal*. I don't think I'd be comfortable with a desk between us...' she said coyly.

'Of course... my place it is, then,' he had responded with smooth alacrity. 'And fortunately I already have champagne on ice...'

Elizabeth sipped the bubbly as she contemplated her nervous dilemma. How did you seduce a man without letting him seduce *you*... especially one as attractive and sexually confident as Jack Hawkwood? If women were throwing themselves at him all the time—as seemed to be the case—he must be extremely blasé and unlikely to easily lose his head. And how did you seduce him without *actually* seducing him? For she had no intention of opening *that* particular Pandora's box of problems for herself. It was *he* who had to be out of control, not her...

Jack let the silence stretch out nerve-rackingly before he rescued her from her quandary by asking softly over the top of his glass, 'Well, Beth, what is this awkward personal matter that you wish to talk about?'

'It's about why I came to the Isle of Hawks...' She looked down at her champagne and idly stirred the bubbles with one finger, thinking that she really should have had the hotel beauty salon do her nails at the same time they'd swept her hair into the sophisticated pleat that had suited her mental image of a vamp. She sucked the sparkling droplets from her finger, looking up just in time to see Jack's tongue touch his upper lip as if he was imitating her action in his thoughts. She flushed, the pretty speech that she had rehearsed all evening evaporating from her head.

'Uncle Simon—I—he's——'

'A private detective?' offered Jack helpfully.

'You know.' Relief swept through her as her suspicions were confirmed. She wasn't betraying anything that wasn't already discovered. 'You probably know the rest of what I'm going to tell you, then.'

'Probably,' he agreed mildly. 'And what I don't know I can make a fairly accurate guess at, but I'd like to hear it in your own words.'

Of course he would. He wanted to rub her nose in her foolishness. She tilted her chin proudly and gave him the edited highlights of the Corvell case, including the initial mix-up at the airport, without mentioning how reluctant a participant she had been. However, she had reckoned without his wicked sense of humour and infuriating intelligence.

'If your uncle thinks you're a good example of a cloak-and-dagger operative,' he commented drily when she finally petered into silence, 'it's a wonder his agency hasn't gone belly up by now. You couldn't have drawn more attention to what you were doing if you'd worn a neon sign. You, *ma chère*, have got a lot to learn about covert operations——'

'Thank you, but I don't *wish* to learn any more!' she snapped, forgetting her supplicant's role.

He tilted his head. 'Lost your taste for excitement already, *chérie*?' he murmured.

She drank her champagne sullenly, feeling that control of the situation was rapidly escaping her uncertain grasp.

'Or was your Uncle Simon just trying to inject some much needed colour and verve into your highly organised existence at some advantage to himself? All work and no play digs Eliza-Beth into a very dull home rut. With your university job and your domestic responsibility for your uncles and their eccentric business you seem to have precious little active social life for an unattached twenty-five-year-old...'

She visibly simmered at his mocking description of her hitherto contented life. 'You *have* been a busy boy,' she said nastily.

Her sarcasm fell very flat. 'Man, *chérie*, man—there's a very important distinction there which I would be enchanted to demonstrate. But I'm sure you wouldn't be here if you hadn't realised *that* ...'

She wasn't entirely sure whether he was referring to her confession of something he already knew or her opinion of his masculinity, so she decided that she might as well take her chances. She leaned forward to set her empty glass on the coffee-table in front of her, aware of the soft light from the lamp falling across her provocative cleavage, the pale swell of her breasts mantled with a faint blush from the long day's unaccustomed exposure to sun and alcohol.

'Oh, I'm sure I've experienced enough social life in my *dull* existence to make my own distinctions,' she said huskily. She slipped off her high-heeled shoes and flexed her legs, tipping her head back against the raised arm of the sofa as she groaned softly. 'Oh, that feels good; those shoes pinch terribly, but they were the only ones that went with my dress.' She half closed her eyes, looking at him through the lashes, a little thrill passing through her at the wickedness of her intent. 'I bought it after I saw it in the window of the hotel boutique this afternoon.'

He could scarcely avoid the compliment she invited, but he made it uniquely and scandalously his own.

'I thought I recognised it. Or is it the body underneath that seems so familiar? Your superb breasts are exquisitely memorable and you have the most beautiful back I've ever seen ... or touched.' He toasted her with his glass, and with a caressing survey that extended from the top of her sleek head to the tips of her toes. 'I think it may have something to do with your paleness, when every other woman in the casino tonight was flaunting a leathery tan. Your legs, too, are wonderfully displayed...but isn't it hot wearing black tights in this climate?'

Trust Jack to so effortlessly discompose her, but Elizabeth was determined not to let him see how bone-deep her blushing reaction went. She had worn black to slim her legs, not to emphasise them, after she had realised that the dress was shorter than it had looked on the mannequin.

'I'm not wearing tights,' she told him archly. 'I find stockings much cooler and ... freer ...'

And with that outrageous comment she lifted her legs and placed her feet boldly across his thighs, lying back against the cushions piled on the end of the couch. 'Would you mind helping iron out the kinks? My feet do ache so from those high heels...'

For a fleeting moment all expression was wiped clean from his face then, wordlessly, he bent and set his own glass down on the floor, and cupped one of her feet with both hands, looking at it with a hungry, sensual curve to his mouth as if he was contemplating taking a bite out of it. Slowly he adjusted his grip, one large hand running caressingly over the top of her foot to bracelet her ankle, the other beginning to knead the tender sole firmly.

'Why do you wear heels if they hurt your feet?'

'I need the extra inches,' she murmured, closing her eyes. She had never had her feet rubbed before and was alarmed at how good it felt.

'Too short, too big... is there anything about yourself that you *are* happy with?' he said wryly, rubbing his fingers along the base of her toes and up underneath them with a rhythmic insistence that made her gasp inaudibly.

'My brain,' she said smartly, to counteract the tingling tendrils of warmth that were darting up her legs.

'Mmm... and what is your brain telling you now, *chérie*?'

He was massaging the ball of her foot, and to her dismay his question was rapidly becoming unanswerable. She opened her eyes, the better to divorce herself from the blissful sensations that were turning the aforesaid brain to mush, and found him watching her.

'Er—that what you're doing feels good,' she said stupidly.

He smiled faintly and only with his mouth, his eyes remaining glitteringly intent. 'And this, does this feel good, too?' he murmured. His hand moved and pressed and something melted deep inside her. With horror Elizabeth wondered if her foot was one of her uncharted erogenous zones, which, given her potentially explosive libido, was quite possible. If so, she had just made an awful mistake.

'F-fine. Great. Er—that's much better, thank you. I think that's enough now——'

She tried to repossess her legs but he prevented her by the simple tactic of splaying the hand on her ankle to encompass both and pinning them firmly against his rock-hard thigh.

'Nonsense,' he purred, 'we're just getting started. Do you know, Beth, that there are some who believe that by massaging certain parts of the soles of the feet you can benefit certain parts of the body...?'

'Really?' she said faintly, more trapped than she would have been if he had captured her hands. With her short skirt she couldn't struggle without subjecting him to flagrant indecency.

'Yes, really. Here, for example. When I press just *here* do you feel a response somewhere else in your body...?' It was auto-suggestion, it had to be, she told herself desperately as his eyes slid to her breasts and they began to ache within the tight confines of her dress.

'No...' Her voice was stifled as she tried to control her breathing.

'Then here...?'

'*No*!' She came up off the cushions, her torso supported on her braced arms, her knees pressed tightly together, legs stiffening.

He knew. Damn it, he *knew* what he was doing to her. It was there in that infuriatingly sensual smile.

'Jack, that's enough——'

'What about here...?'

'*Jack*!' His hand caressed the sole of her foot once more and slid abruptly up the underside of her stockinged calf, cupping the rounded flesh briefly before stroking up to the back of her knee. Her legs automatically bent to escape the sizzling contact, her narrow skirt riding dangerously up her thighs, her imprisoned feet twisting more deeply into his lap as she tried to jerk them free.

She stilled, a wild warmth flushing her body as she registered the hardness nestling against her heels that was not his thigh. Her toes curled involuntarily, scrunching the dark fabric covering his inner thigh as she realised that he was not the cool, controlled tormentor of her frightened imagination, that he was as aroused by the game she had instigated as she had been ... perhaps more so.

Suddenly her misplaced confidence came rushing back. If she was trapped then so was he—far more obviously so. Why, he was practically seducing himself. This was going to be like taking candy from a baby!

She stopped trying to wrest herself away from his hold and tilted her head back, her lips parting, an expression of unconscious and very feminine cunning crossing her face, making her look as sultry as the archetypal vamp she had been attempting to emulate.

Warily Jack removed his hands from her legs, not taking his eyes off hers, watching the violet gaze become dark and heavy-lidded. Instead of taking advantage of her freedom Elizabeth flexed her feet experimentally. The breath came hissing through his teeth.

'Eliza-Beth.'

Now it was his turn to admonish in a slow drawl that hinted of darker passions. She pouted, her small pink mouth an erotic counterpoint to the huge purple eyes.

'Yes, Jack?' she enquired innocently. She moved her feet again and a low rumble vibrated in his chest and his hands clenched into fists on his thighs.

'What are you doing?'

'Waiting for you to finish my foot massage.'

'I thought you'd cried "enough".'

He sounded wry, but his expression was anything but. Even with his tan she could see the dark blood that had risen in his face, the faint flare to his nostrils with each rapid inhalation.

'It's a woman's prerogative to change her mind.' She relaxed her arms and leaned back against the arm of the couch again, in an attitude of conscious abandon. Having spent years successfully repressing her powerful sexual urges, Elizabeth was finding the freedom of provocative man-woman banter a headily addictive experience.

'Do you really want me to continue what I was doing?'

He might have relinquished control of his body but he was some way from losing his head. Elizabeth needed his thoughts as clouded as her own had been a few moments ago.

'Don't you want to?' she asked, her normally husky voice made even deeper by her tense throat.

'I think it's very evident what I want.' He glanced down at her feet in his lap with a twisted smile. 'But I'm not a foot-fetishist—to get it I'd need to be lying between your thighs rather than your heels...unless of course you're a particularly gymnastic lover...'

'*Jack*!' Just when she settled into her vamping role, he shocked her back into prudery.

'Well, darling, you did ask...' And to her further shock he grasped her ankles suddenly, lifting them from his lap and parting them far enough to make a space for himself as he turned in one lightning-swift motion to brace himself over her. He lay, his hips aligned with the hem of her skirt, which was pulled taut between her sprawled legs, his powerful arms caging her as he laughed into her flushed face.

'What's the matter, *chérie*? Bitten off more than you can chew?'

'I'd certainly like to bite you,' she burst out, temper mingling with a riot of desire.

His eyelids dropped. 'Mmm, exciting...you did that once before and I found it quite violently erotic. This time, though, I want you to take my clothes off first...'

Elizabeth's eyes widened, appalled and fascinated by the feverishly escalating indecency of the conversation. Not even in her most shamefully abandoned moments with Ryan had she invited such an explicit ravishment of words...but then Ryan had always been intent on controlling her fervour, rather than feeding it. He had never openly praised her body, preferring more cerebral compliments, and he had been a silent, serious lover. He had never confused her by blowing constantly hot and cold, always maintaining an elegant evenness of temperament that Elizabeth had adoringly tried to pattern herself on.

Ryan had been an intellectual whereas Jack was very much a decisive man of action, a fighter and a gambler, definitely not the kind of man that Elizabeth would normally contemplate any kind of relationship with, no matter how attractive. But the situation was most emphatically *not* normal, and although she could not afford to become involved with him it was necessary that he *think* she might. For a while at least she must give in to the forbidden allure of a dangerous liaison. And anyway, a little voice murmured in the wicked depths of her brain, after this abortive holiday was over she would never see him again. Whatever happened between them, no one but the two of them would ever know...

Elizabeth's breathing shortened in the knowledge of what she was thinking, her limbs felt heavy suddenly...languid and weakly passive. Her hands, which had been clutched nervously to her breast, slid limply to her sides, palms opening beside her almost bare shoulders. She waited, curious, to see what he would dare do next...

'Do you know what the first rule of the game is, according to Ovid?'

Elizabeth had to moisten her lips to allow her dry mouth to work.

'No.' How could he expect her to worry about the wafflings of a centuries-dead Roman poet when she could feel the rise and fall of his chest lightly tantalising her breasts?

Jack shifted, his hip wedging against her inner thigh as he took his weight on one arm, and lifted the other to run his finger over her damp mouth as he told her with a lazy sexual arrogance, 'Women can always be caught.'

Elizabeth was wildly aroused but she wasn't entirely lost to her female pride. 'So can men,' she countered huskily.

'So we can. So I suppose it boils down to who is more eager to do the catching in each individual case. Who is being caught here, Beth? You, or me?'

She vaguely sensed some trap that she needed to be wary of. 'I don't know, maybe we both are,' she said vaguely, as she wondered how different his hard mouth would taste when flavoured by champagne.

'So you see us as equals, then? I like that. It means fewer recriminations later,' he murmured cryptically. The hand moved from her mouth to lightly encircle her throat, then it tunnelled under the nape of her neck to pull at the pins that held her sophisticated hairstyle in place.

'The smooth swept-back look doesn't suit you,' he told her, as he fanned the dark, rippling waves across the white leather behind her head. 'You should let your hair flow loose and untamed ... like your body. There wasn't a man there tonight who didn't look at you in that scrap of black silk and want you. But you only looked back at one. Me.'

His eyes were dark with a triumphant satisfaction that made Elizabeth quiver. 'And you didn't put on that sinful dress and shrug off several hundred thousand francs just because you wanted to *talk*, did you, Beth? That's the kind of dress a woman wears when she's feeling reckless, not when she wants to impress with her honesty. So what is it you *really* want from me tonight . . . ?'

He was much too lucid for her to answer that question just yet. Elizabeth shifted slightly within the cage of his body, her stockinged leg rubbing against his.

'Don't you know? And I thought you were a perceptive man,' she taunted huskily. The fingers of one hand curved nervously into her palm as she reached out with the other to trace the hard curve of his jaw. Then, imitating his action of a few moments ago, she slid her fingers into his hair and raked it loose from the narrow black band.

His eyes narrowed to silver slits as his head moved down until he was just a kiss away. 'You want me untamed too, Eliza-Beth? You have decided to stop fighting yourself and seek the pleasure that you know I can give you?'

Such beautiful, breathtaking arrogance. Damn it, didn't he ever stop asking questions and just *accept* . . . ? Elizabeth's impatience burst the bounds of her control and her hand flattened against his scalp, tugging him that last, precious inch.

He didn't taste any different, only better, the flavour of him melting over her tongue, the first sip only exacerbating the hunger that drove her to wind both arms around his neck and twist her mouth under his, needing the co-operation that was strangely lacking. Oh, God, was her desperate eagerness turning him off? She tensed as the old feeling of shame impinged on her consciousness.

As if her wavering doubt communicated itself to him Jack suddenly threw off his passiveness and took full command of the intimate embrace, his hand cupping her jaw as he plunged his tongue into her mouth, biting and sucking at the soft innermost recesses with a gentle savagery that utterly shattered her former notions of what a kiss could be. His hair, freed from her fingers, curtained their joined mouths, shrouding them in a private world of cleanly fragrant darkness.

'Oh!' When his mouth broke away from hers she was bereft, but only until she felt the warm, moist progression down the arch of her throat to the V of her collarbone. She sighed with pleasure as the brush of his mouth was accompanied by the silky stroke of his hair, like the stroke of a fur glove on her sensitive skin.

'You like that, *chérie*?' He marched a little string of kisses over the twin swells of her breasts, just above the line of black fabric that hid their full splendour from his view. Elizabeth arched slightly, fighting the restriction of the tight skirt that trapped her extended legs outside his, yearning for more. He re-traced the kisses, this time taking small, stinging bites of the rosy flesh.

'Oh!'

'Is that all you can say?' His voice was thick with teasing passion at her wordless cry. 'For such a well read woman you're a very inarticulate lover, *chérie*. Don't you want to tell me what you're feeling, what I should do?'

'I didn't realise you needed instruction,' Elizabeth gasped shakily as he licked and sucked at the tiny red marks his teeth had grazed upon her skin. Inside the black silk her breasts felt unbearably hot and tight, the nipples chafing against their luxurious wrapping. Why, oh, why wouldn't he touch her *properly* ... as he must know that she *needed* to be touched? She was afraid that if she tried to use words she wouldn't be able to stop, that the helpless tide of her feelings would flood away with her. Soon she would make *him* say the words that she had planned to seduce from him, but for now she just wanted to steal something for herself... She couldn't tell him, but she could *show* him...

Her eyes deepened from violet to indigo as she fiercely attacked the pearl buttons of his shirt, operating purely on touch as his bent head masked her sight, his skilled mouth still rousing her aching frustration.

'Easy, darling,' he murmured, as she tried to pull the edges of his shirt apart before it was fully unbuttoned. 'Here, let me.' He knelt to shed his cuff-links and peel off the offending garment, grasping her by the waist and holding her still as she would have arched up painfully to press herself against his hair-roughened chest. 'You predicted I would lose my shirt tonight, didn't you, *chérie*?' he stated with gravelly satisfaction as he looked down at her lush body. 'I wouldn't have objected to playing if I'd known you meant it so literally.'

'Please...' Dizziness swam in her head as she pleaded for deliverance. His grip on her waist was so tight that she thought she was going to faint, his fingers wrapping around her back to splay across her bare skin, his thumbs pressing into her belly, testing its firm resilience, causing a scalding heat to pool there.

'Please what?' he whispered, his hands moving obligingly from her waist to rest on her parted thighs, sliding slowly up under the taut black silk hem to stroke the borderline where stocking met tender satin skin.

'Oh!' She arched convulsively, forgetting the naïve limits she had set for how far she would let him go, forgetting everything but the intense pleasure exploding through her senses, sending her nervous system into total overload.

'Please what?' His fingers pressed under the suspender straps, lightly tugging them in a way that pulled at muscles deep inside her abdomen. She felt hot and cold both at once and marvellously alive in a way she never had before.

'Oh, don't——' she begged, as his marvellous hands moved away again and hovered, as if he was wondering what part of her to torture with pleasure next. She put her hands on his shoulders, feeling them thicken and bunch as she unconsciously guided him.

'Don't what? Do this?' This time his finger hooked into the indiscreet slit in the centre of her bodice and created a wicked tension as he pulled, lifting her towards him. He bent and inhaled the fragrant heat that rose from between her breasts. Her eyes closed, her head fell back and his murmur was like tearing silk in her ears. 'Tell me... tell me everything you like, Eliza-Beth, every wish, every fantasy and I'll give it to you... all of it... anything, everything you want...'

'A-anything?' Elizabeth knew that there was a proper answer for that, something she was prepared to say, but then his finger exerted an ounce more pressure and she felt the ruffle on her bodice scrape one rigid nipple, exposing it to the cool night air. And his mouth... it was... soon he would... and it would be too late...

'I don't... I want——' Her mind struggled to reassert its ascendancy over the tumultuous revolution of her body, capable only of dealing in the simplest of one-syllable concepts. 'Time...'

His breath was exquisitely damp and hot on her swollen nipple.

'Time?'

The temptation to deny her brief return to sanity was almost overwhelming. The need for that moist, intimate caress was excruciatingly intense. 'I...yes.'

'Time for what?'

'I—I don't remember...' Opening her eyes had been a mistake. He filled her vision, rearing over her—big, powerful, starkly aroused, his face raw with disbelief and a smouldering sexual anger. He was wild for her, she realised achingly, tenderly, and in a way that Ryan had never been. She would never compare the two men again. 'Jack——' She touched his cheek and he snapped his head to the side, and bit her finger.

'Ouch!' She jerked back and struggled to sit up. 'That hurt!'

'Let me make it better,' he growled savagely, grabbing her fluttering hand and placing her stinging finger in his mouth. He sucked strongly, rhythmically, and she shivered at the explicitness of the act that was designed to dominate rather than soothe.

'Better?' He let her go and smiled into her glazed purple eyes, a dangerous, feral smile that was still on his lips when he bent and did the same to her peaked nipple, pulling the bodice down so that he had complete access to the rosy ripeness, taking it roughly between his teeth and teasing it with his tongue before drawing it deep into his scalding mouth.

Her hoarse cry of shock and pleasure seemed to appease his desire to punish, for the powerful wet suction settled to a slow, leisurely suckling that was devastatingly effective at re-establishing his supremacy.

She was drenched with blinding delight as he paid equally lavish attention to her other breast and suddenly nothing mattered any more but pleasing him as he was pleasing her, loving and being loved as she had longed to be in her most secret dreams, fiercely and without inhibition, by a man who gloried in the violence of her strongly passionate nature.

But not completely mindlessly. As his fingers wrenched at the concealed zip in the side of her dress, Jack forced her to meet his hotly arrogant gaze.

'Yes?'

She blazed her answer at him. Even to ask was an unendurable delay. 'Yes, oh, *yes* . . .'

She raged like a storm in his arms, one that he rode in a triumphant frenzy of desire, tearing off their clothes as his body melted into hers, his groans and wild, erotic urgings spurring her further, faster, deeper towards the heart of the whirlwind that had turbulently engulfed them both. The first convulsive paroxysm of pleasure barely checked his extravagant pace as he pursued her from peak to peak until she cried out in an ecstasy of exhaustion.

He rolled on to his side and pulled her body hard against him until her trembling eased, his skin as slick and moist as the leather beneath them. His breathing was ragged and harsh as he rubbed her tender back with his big hand, but when he finally spoke it wasn't to utter words of love.

'Sex can be a formidable weapon, *chérie*, *if* you can wield it with the proper detachment. You can't,' he added ruthlessly. 'You never will. You're too easily aroused—— No!' He muffled her protest by smothering her mouth with a rough kiss. 'I don't mean in the sense of being promiscuous, I mean because your responses are too honest, you're too sensuous a woman to be cold and calculating, too honourable to be comfortable with deception—your feelings and emotions will ultimately always give you away.'

She shuddered with despair at the awful thought and he tilted her head with a firm hand under her chin so that he could see her face.

His voice gentled at her bewildered misery. 'Is that why you suddenly got cold feet, Beth? Because you were afraid of the intensity of what you were feeling? But now you know that you have nothing to be afraid of with me as your lover. There need be no more barriers between us...'

Elizabeth guiltily avoided his eyes as she pulled out of his softened grasp and scrambled off the couch, hastily pulling on her panties and dress, stuffing her stockings into her small clutch-bag and smoothing out the creases in her skirt, wishing she could as easily straighten out her confused tangle of emotions regarding this man. Her body aching with sweet satiation, she couldn't regret what had happened, but where did they go from here?

There was nowhere to go. He wasn't asking for her love and she mustn't offer it. She wanted him more than she had ever wanted anyone—or anything—before in her whole life. But there were too many strikes against them—not the least that he thought that she was *honourable*. The compliment made her ill when she thought about how she was abusing *his* trust, *his* honour. He would hate her when he found out and hopefully the weight of his contempt would crush whatever foolish seeds their glorious lovemaking had planted in her heart. She flushed at the uneasy knowledge that in hiding the truth from him she was also trying to hide from herself...

She was so lost in her silent agony that she didn't notice his curiosity sharpen at her transparently guilty expression and the dreaming sadness with which she attempted to banish the disordered evidence of their lovemaking. Slowly he followed her example, waiting until she was edging for the door before saying abruptly, 'How would you like to spend the day with me again tomorrow?'

His question was so far from what she had expected that Elizabeth gaped at him. 'Tomorrow?'

'The day following this night,' he clarified limpidly.

'Tomorrow?' She couldn't believe what he was suggesting. 'But... tomorrow aren't you having lunch with your grandfather?'

It was said in tones of such riveting casualness that Jack almost laughed, except all of a sudden he was not feeling half as amused as he had a few moments before.

'So I am.' His voice was lightly musing, as if considering the matter.

Now Elizabeth knew how a prostitute felt. She had sold the temporary use of her body for this moment and now she had to force herself to take the unexpected opportunity for payment.

'Perhaps I could come with you,' she said timidly. 'I mean, I'd be very interested in seeing the St Clair estate...'

'Yes, I remember you expressing your interest on the way over from the mainland,' he murmured, and Elizabeth discovered she was winding her fingers nervously in her hair. Hurriedly she put her shaking hands behind her back.

'However, I think I mentioned my grandfather's been ill. He's not up to meeting strangers.'

'Oh.' Say something, Elizabeth. Give him a pout and say, 'Darling, after tonight surely I'm not a stranger...'

Elizabeth's hands wrung nervously behind her back, wondering whether it was a good sign that Jack didn't seem to be subjecting her to his interrogating stare. He was looking thoughtfully past her... into the mirror that she had failed to notice on the opposite side of the room.

Finally Elizabeth forced herself to make the only decision she could. The honour of the Lambs had to come first. She might have fallen *in* love with Jack but she *loved* her family. She stopped wringing and firmly crossed the fingers of her concealed left hand.

'I wouldn't disturb your grandfather. I'd be happy to just have a look around the house and grounds...'

'Would you?' he murmured, still staring absently over her shoulder.

She crossed the fingers of her right hand, for extra protection. 'Of course.' She swallowed as his eyes suddenly swivelled back to her face. 'And it would mean we could spend some more time t-together...'

She tailed off nervously at the look in his narrowed eyes, a hard, predatory, sinister look that seemed to strip-mine her soul. When he nodded slowly, conceding her victory, she heard the hollow ring.

A slithering coil of excitement tightened in her stomach as she shakily escaped back to her own half of the bungalow. She had a feeling that she hadn't even *begun* to pay the price of her folly—and the awful thing was that she was actually looking forward to it!

CHAPTER NINE

THE St Clair estate was as magnificent as rumour and hearsay had led her to expect, but for Elizabeth it wasn't the beauty of the extensively landscaped grounds or the elegance of the French architecture that captured her imagination—it was the library.

It had taken her nearly an hour of wandering through the procession of exquisitely furnished rooms on the ground floor to find it: two rooms packed floor to ceiling with books, some in temperature-controlled cases, others in meticulously arranged shelves and at least a third of the superb collection in a shambolic stack which suggested that the cataloguer had lost interest in the job halfway through.

Elizabeth's hands tightened on the strap of her heavy bag. She could slip the books out and back on a shelf now and no one would be any the wiser. If they had been missed it would be thought they had merely been misplaced. At least then she would only have the necklace to worry about.

She looked around the cavernous room nervously, touching the necklace beneath her prim floral blouse. Wearing it had taken on the nature of a penance that she was fated to perform. Whenever she took it off— even when she watched it go straight into the huge hotel safe—she suffered severe anxiety verging on physical pain about the possibility of it being lost or stolen. She had been braced to keep Jack at arm's length this morning, or at least from around her neck, but to her chagrin he had been blandly circumspect, collecting her from her doorstep for all the world as if they were teenagers going out on an innocent first date rather than a man and woman who had made passionate love together only a few hours before. The drive to the estate had taken little over twenty minutes in the small hotel buggy and all the way Jack had chatted easily about the island's history and entertained her with stories about the tradition-bound St Clair family's more eccentric members, who apparently included his grandfather. Gradually his casualness had the desired effect, and Elizabeth was able to push the vivid memory of her embarrassingly fierce response to his lovemaking aside in favour of the simple pleasure of enjoying his company.

Seeing the smooth, high concrete wall and barred iron gates that had to be opened by a guard before they could enter the tree-lined avenue to the flamboyant St Clair residence and the impressive alarm system, Elizabeth had come to the rueful conclusion that she would never have got into the place on her own. The only practical way in was the way she had come, by personal invitation.

If only her acceptance had been as innocent as the invitation. Glancing over the locked toughened-glass cases and spotting a rare fifteenth-century thirty-six-line Bible, of which she knew that there were only fifteen in existence—the latest having been auctioned at Christie's for 1.1 million pounds—Elizabeth felt faint with relief that something like *that* hadn't been involved. No wonder the place was well protected and casual callers discouraged. She opened her bag and was reaching inside when someone spoke behind her.

'I thought I might find you in here.'

'Jack!' She whirled around, snapping the bag closed, her hand pressed against her frantically beating heart. 'W-why did you think that?' she managed to ask lightly. He had told her that she was free to explore while he sought his grandfather's room to inform him of their presence.

'With your fascination for books, where else would you gravitate but towards the library?' he answered smoothly.

'It's magnificent,' she murmured, bringing her ragged breathing under control. 'How's your grandfather?'

'Isn't it?' He ignored her question and waved a hand at the shelves. 'And all these have been acquired since the war. Most of *Grandpère*'s original collection went up in smoke when the château was bombed. Some of these are bulk-lots bought from other collectors trying to make good their own war losses ... or, more recently, their stock market ones. However, *Grandpère* knows that Jean-Jules and I don't share his abiding passion for old books, so he's decided to sell off all except a core of his treasured favourites while he's still capable of doing it himself ... only to carefully selected, personally approved buyers, of course.'

Elizabeth smiled involuntarily. 'He sounds just like my uncles ...' She hesitated, wondering how much he knew.

In deference to his grandfather's old-fashioned ideas of proper dress, Jack was wearing a pale grey suit and tie, and yet he still looked coolly casual as he thrust one hand into his pockets and regarded her with a whimsical smile.

'Probably why they all got on so well. Over the past few months my grandfather has invited quite a number of prospective buyers here to express their interest in his collection. I didn't realise until he recognised your name that your uncles had been among them. Why didn't you tell me? I would have better understood your interest in the estate...'

Elizabeth's face pinkened. 'I—I didn't realise you were even related until yesterday and then, well... I didn't want to presume on what was after all a very brief acquaintanceship,' she finished lamely.

He strolled over and took her hand, politely not commenting on the pounding pulse as he raised her wrist to his mouth. 'Are you talking about us or our elders? In future, feel free to presume, *ma chère*,' he murmured. 'My grandfather remembers your uncles well.'

'Oh, really?' Her pulse erupted even more furiously and she struggled to keep him at arm's length. Why 'well'? Because he suspected them of being ageing con men?

'Yes. They talked quite a bit about you. They're very proud of their clever niece, perhaps even a tiny bit intimidated by your managing ways.' He let her go and idly circled the room, forcing her to turn to keep him in her sight.

How she hated that word—intimidated. 'Someone has to be practical. Most of the time they exist in a world of their own,' she said stiffly.

'I think I used the wrong word,' he murmured, alert to the flicker of pain that crossed her face. 'I should have said they're a little in awe of you. They know without you to take charge their business would have gone to rack and ruin some time ago, but they also told my grandfather that they were worried that your devotion to them was jeopardising your chances of marrying and having a family of our own.'

Elizabeth looked at him, shocked. 'They've never said anything like that to me,' she said defensively.

Jack grinned. 'I think they were well into *Grandpère*'s fine stock of brandy at the time, and talk was fast and loose. I don't doubt that *Grandpère* responded by bemoaning the fact that I haven't yet done my duty and married a nice girl who will bear Hawkwood heirs and curtail my regrettable independence of spirit.'

'But surely your brother's children are the Hawkwood heirs...' Elizabeth was relieved that the conversation had moved off the subject of herself.

'In the strict sense yes, although not as far as this place is concerned. This he intends to leave to us jointly, but Jules and Marie-Clare—that's Jules wife—' with a little sidelong glance that mocked her puzzled ignorance '—prefer not to reside permanently in a "sub-tropical backwater". As you might guess, the distance in that marriage is not only in kilometres. I don't approve, but neither can I condemn. Being the younger, I was never pressured to make a dynastic marriage. If our positions had been reversed——' he shrugged '—who knows? Perhaps I too would have settled for a civilised "arrangement".'

'I can't quite see you "settling" for anything,' Elizabeth blurted, and he bowed teasingly.

'I shall accept that as a compliment. To continue: therefore I will be the one to actually live here, as master of our joint inheritance . . .'

'You'll move out of the hotel? Live here, all by yourself?' It was a strangely distasteful vision to think of him alone here, living in the solitary splendour. Even though Jack gave the impression of being sufficient unto himself he enjoyed himself so richly in his role of autocratic and gregarious hotelier that Elizabeth could not imagine him being happy with the kind of isolation that obviously suited his grandfather. He had too much energy, too intense an enjoyment of life to want to retreat from it, either physically or mentally.

He gave her a heavy-lidded smile. 'I hope not *entirely* alone, *chérie*. *Grandpère* is only seventy-five. With reasonable care for his delicate health, I hope he will live a number of years yet. He is a fighter and he'll not let go of life easily. By that time—who is to say?—I may be deep in the blissful toils of domesticity, father to a brood of children who will fill these echoing halls with their life and laughter . . .'

It was an almost poetically beautiful vision. 'You want children?' Elizabeth asked.

'I almost had one, once,' he said quietly, looking out of the window over the immaculately rolled lawn that sloped down to a perfect slice of beach. 'Zenobia was pregnant with my child when she was killed.'

'Oh, Jack. I'm so sorry.' She moved over to touch his straight back tentatively. The impulse to wrap herself around him and cry took her by surprise. Her own life crises seemed petty and unimportant in comparison with all that he had endured.

'I would have loved the child,' he continued, without acknowledging her touch, 'whatever I had discovered the mother to be. I don't subscribe to the theory of visiting the sins of the parents on their offspring.'

Or the sins of the uncles? Elizabeth was appalled at the callous opportunism of the thought that bubbled to the surface of her mind. If she confided in him now he would think that she was using his deeply personal grief for her own gain. And perhaps he would be right...

He turned and caught her in the midst of mental self-disgust.

'Don't look so tragic, Eliza-Beth, I did my mourning long ago. Now I look to the future. And you, do you wish for the loving husband and children that your uncles are anxious that you are depriving yourself of?'

The wish that did rise instantly in her mind was so far beyond her reach that it was foolish in the extreme. Her eyes shuttered against the pain of it. 'Some day, I suppose...'

'Some day?' His tone mused on her feeble attempt at indifference. 'That is very vague from a woman who seems to pride herself on independence and decisiveness. Should I assume, therefore, that your experience of love was as bitter in its way as mine, and that it has made you wary of being hurt again?'

'It wasn't love,' she said jerkily, unable to stop the words of denial bubbling out. 'I was very young—nineteen. I only thought I was in love but it was an infatuation. A *physical* infatuation,' she stressed with a pointed look in his direction.

'So it was your first affair. And he was a hot-blooded young student?'

'No, as matter of fact he was in his late thirties ... one of my professors ...'

'Ah, a father-figure.' He nodded gravely.

'Definitely not. He was very good-looking, very sexy,' she snapped.

'A good lover?'

She blushed and frowned at his boldness. 'It was a long time ago.'

He smiled wickedly. 'Not a memorable one, then— I have no need to worry that you're making unflattering comparisons. Was he a modern Casanova, cutting a swath through his students and ducking any threat of commitment?'

From the perspective of maturity she could laugh. Strangely enough, it no longer hurt to remember. 'No, definitely *not* a Casanova ... he wanted commitment but with someone less—er—physically *exuberant* ...'

Realisation kindled in the silver eyes. They glowed with a savage condemnation—but not of her.

'Ah ... *now* I see ... So *he* was the one responsible for this excruciating self-consciousness about your body. You were too much a woman, even as a girl, for him to handle. So to salve his wounded ego he made you feel uncomfortable with your sexuality, made you doubt the honesty of your emotions? And you *believed* this?'

She stirred uneasily. He made it all sound so simple, but it wasn't. 'I was rather embarrassingly intense at that age——'

'But surely your other lovers——'

'Not everyone bounces from bed to bed as light-heartedly as you do!' she cut him off furiously.

There was a tiny silence as he digested the implications of her remark. Then, 'Light-hearted? Now *you* use the wrong word, I think. Jealous, *chérie?*'

She glared at him. 'Yes.'

For a moment he was taken aback by her reckless honesty. Then his shock melted into a creamy satisfaction. 'You have no need to be. I'm not my brother. I enjoy sex but I have never been indiscriminate, and pain and betrayal evidently have an extremely depressive effect on my libido because last night was my first with a woman for a long time...'

He took a step towards her and Elizabeth backed away, so he stopped, 'I don't want to talk about last night,' she choked.

'I rather gathered that,' he murmured wryly, referring to the aloofness with which she had greeted him that morning. 'But some time soon we must settle this thing between us. Just let me say this: I am very proud to be your lover. I have never in my life so thoroughly enjoyed making love to a woman as much as I did last night, with you.

'Now...' He strode briskly to the door, as if he hadn't just pierced her heart with the most graceful and erotic compliment she had ever received. Even if it wasn't true, he made her believe that *he* believed it so...

'Why don't I show you around some of the upstairs galleries?' he continued. 'If you're interested in French Impressionists we have quite an array——'

'I haven't had a chance to really look around here yet...' Elizabeth faltered, hanging back.

He held the door open, giving her a hard stare that transferred itself around the room. 'What is it you want to see?'

'Nothing special,' she said, joining him hurriedly. 'I just thought I'd browse. Perhaps I can come back by myself while you're having lunch, now that I know the way...'

'*We're* having lunch on the north terrace after I've shown you upstairs and then, if you've brought your suit as I suggested, we can have a swim...'

'Are—am I joining you and your grandfather for lunch, then?' Elizabeth murmured faintly, as he ushered her away from the library's myriad temptations. 'How is he? You didn't say...'

'Didn't I? Not well, I'm afraid. He won't be able to lunch with me after all.'

'Oh, I'm sorry. I hope he'll be all right,' said Elizabeth anxiously, her concern more for the man striding up the stairs beside her than for her own dilemma. Every time he mentioned his grandfather it was with a respect that was touchingly reverent in such a tough, cynical man.

He explained why during their leisurely lunch on the terrace overlooking the sea, having taken an almost boyish delight in impressing her with the breathtaking splendour of his home.

Alain St Clair had been a member of the French Resistance and had been captured and tortured by the *Gestapo*. Although there had been no outward scarring, the long-term effects had been debilitating, his weakened heart curtailing the drive and determination with which he had reconstructed his heritage. His young son having died in a concentration camp along

with his mother, Alain had pinned his hopes for a new
dynasty on his only son-in-law, Jack's father, who had
proved not only a supremely successful businessman,
but also a successful breeder of sons. Jack freely admitted that he was glad to be the second son. Although as a youth he had been somewhat jealous of the
attention showered on Jean-Jules, as an adult he had
deeply appreciated the freedom to forge his own life.

At the information that his grandfather had a weak
heart Elizabeth's own sank miserably, weighed down
by the guilty millstone around her neck. No wonder
Jack was so protective. Even if she did manage to escape his vigilant attention long enough to see Alain St
Clair alone, what if the shock was too great for the old
man's frail constitution?

She pushed away a delicious concoction of tropical
fruits chilled in liqueur that an unobtrusive servant had
placed in front of her and picked up her cup of coffee,
staring into its black and bitter depths.

What was she to do?

She knew what she *should* do.

Tell him. Trust him. Take the risk that Jack's sense
of fairness would override his fury and disgust. Hope
that he had meant what he said about last night, and
that the memory would soften any thoughts of punishment or revenge. Surely by now he must know her
well enough to realise that she was innocent of malicious intent.

How? She had lied to him, actively and by omis-
sion, again and again.

The only time she had told him the truth was when
she had run out of lies to serve her purpose. And she
had seduced him. Deliberately. And pretended to her-

self that it was in the line of duty. Another lie. She had fallen in love with him, but he wouldn't believe that either. Not now.

He had been betrayed once before by a woman who had been his lover.

But he had loved her. Perhaps he would be more lenient on a woman he could only have intended having a brief affair with...

She touched her throat, as if the precious metal there was a talisman against the wrath of its owner. 'Jack——'

'You're not on the contraceptive pill for medical reasons, are you, *chérie*?'

She stared across the table at him, wide-eyed with shock, her coffee-cup clattering in its saucer.

'I merely ask because lovers should be frank about such things,' he said calmly, biting into a piece of juicy gold pineapple. 'You have been celibate for some years, therefore I presume you haven't needed to take any precautions about having your "some day" family arrive unexpectedly soon.'

Elizabeth sucked in a ragged breath as the true recklessness of her behaviour the previous night hit her between the eyes. Everything blurred but the dark face with its unexpectedly gentle expression.

'I don't—I wouldn't—I didn't——'

'Fortunately I did,' he interrupted kindly, selecting another segment of fruit.

'What?'

'You don't remember?'

'N-no...' The whole experience had melted together in her mind into one glorious white-hot mass of exquisite sensation. Even to think about it sent tiny thrills of delight darting up and down the most sensitive parts of her body.

He leaned back in the dainty wrought-iron chair. 'Never mind, *chérie*,' he said caressingly. 'I am glad that I obviously didn't break the mood for you. Suffice it to say that I protected you last night as I will tonight and all the nights to come if you wish me to...'

If she *wished*? 'Tonight?' she questioned huskily.

'Yes. I think you will be far more comfortable here than at the hotel. And we shall be more private, too.'

It took a moment before she realised what he meant. 'You want me to stay *here*?'

'Not want,' he corrected her punctiliously, 'we *are* staying here. I have already asked *Grandpère* if he would not object, and delegated my responsibilities at the hotel for this evening...'

'But—I have nothing to wear,' was the most coherent, and prosaic, of the objections screaming in her brain.

His reaction was a piratical smile and a drawl that turned her to fire. 'What a delicious thought, *chérie*, but as it happens I have asked for all your things to be brought to us here.'

'*All* my things? How long are we going to stay?'

He didn't comment on her tacit capitulation and resumed enjoying his fruit salad. 'As long as it takes, Eliza-Beth.'

'As long as what takes?'

'Why, for you to realise that I am a man who can be trusted.'

With what? Her body? Her heart? 'You hold my passport, I have to trust you,' she pointed out truculently.

With the air of a magician producing a rabbit, Jack reached into the inner pocket of his jacket and withdrew a slim dark blue folder and placed it on the table between them. The effect was all he could have wished for. Elizabeth stared at it, round-eyed, and then at him. She made no move to touch it.

'Do you want to leave, Beth?'

'You mean here?'

'I mean me. This place, this island,' he added carelessly as if the latter two were the less important.

She paled, emphasising the conflict in her dark eyes. 'I—I don't know.'

He was quick to prey on her weakness. 'As usual you evade an answer, so I will give it for you. You don't want to leave. You cannot because you are here for a reason...and not the one you so prettily confessed last night to soften me up for your clumsy attempt at seduction. It is something to do with this house and your book-buying uncles and my grandfather. I got sidetracked for a while by your ridiculous detective mission for your other uncle—who I might comment is a little casual about his security. But I was always aware of some deeper game in play, for stakes I suspect are far more serious. You obviously wanted to come here, so I decided to bring you. We will stay.'

'If I was so "clumsy" I'm surprised you could bring yourself to succumb to my seduction!' Elizabeth flared, stricken by his unexpectedly brutal volte-face, just when she had been on the verge of being truly honest with him.

'Do not make me pay for another man's sins, *chérie*. To succumb means to give way in the face of overwhelming force or desire, does it not?' His precise mastery of English reminded her that it was not his first language. 'In our case I think the succumbing was very mutual. And I too was clumsy in my eagerness to make you mine.' If that was clumsiness Elizabeth went faint at the prospect of experiencing his idea of finesse!

'The evening ended precisely as I had always intended it should end. I had waited long enough for you to conquer your shyness. And I was pleased to find out that you are not at all shy in bed. You are earthy and generous. I liked your frank delight in our coupling, the sounds you made when I ripped away your control, the sight of you climaxing so sweetly under me——'

'*Jack*!' Elizabeth's cry was a scandalised whisper. In spite of the fact that the servants had withdrawn she blushed at the thought that his bold voice might carry.

'What? I am too *unsubtle* for you, *ma chère*?' He pinned her with his challenging grey stare. 'You hide so much from me, but this you cannot hide, thank God. Passion does not belong only in bed. That is for misers and stagnant professors. If you stay, I will teach you that passion belongs in every room of the house and that it is a full-blooded shout of victory rather than a whisper of shame. Whatever else happens between us, we can have this...'

It sounded utterly wonderful.

She took a deep breath and picked up her passport. He straightened in his chair and she saw that he was not as confident as he sounded.

She put the passport in her bag, trying not to look at the three books cushioned in tissue-paper which resided accusingly there.

'I'll stay,' she said defiantly, and then temporised, 'But only for a little while.' She couldn't bring herself to put a definite date to the end of this reckless enchantment but unlike her last love-affair this time she would not be entering it in a mist of rosy optimism.

He seemed gravely satisfied with her less than passionate declaration, treating her as tenderly as if she had just laid her heart at his feet. And perhaps she had, she thought glumly.

They swam and lazed away the afternoon and when evening came Elizabeth changed for dinner in a room that was, surprisingly, some distance away from Jack's.

He had grinned wickedly at her confusion when she had realised that the adjoining door in her room led only into a thankfully modern bathroom.

'We must observe the proprieties, *ma chère*,' he murmured, stroking her hot cheek with one finger. '*Grandpère* is old-fashioned in his expectations of the behaviour of his guests, even if they happen to be family. We dress for dinner and if we aren't married we must sneak through the hallways at night to our secret liaisons in the approved romantic fashion.'

'Does he know——?'

'That we are lovers?' He rescued her from her embarrassment. 'I did not tell him so, but for all his years he is a very shrewd old man. Doubtless the music of your name on my tongue gave him a hint of my feelings.'

She wished he would give *her* such a hint. As it was she could only allow herself to assume that his flattering intensity was the result of his highly developed hunting instinct—the excitement of pursuit followed by the triumphant climax of capture.

When he tapped at her door to take her down to dinner and Elizabeth opened it to find him in dark formal wear rather than the tropical white he usually wore at the casino, she was glad that she had chosen the simple bottle-green dress with a high cowl-necked bodice sweeping in an A-line to the hem of a calf-length skirt. Its clever design almost rendered her figure demure. She had also put her hair up, although she knew he preferred it free. Tonight she didn't want to be blatantly seductive. Tonight she just wanted to be herself.

He passed the test with flying colours, his approval evident in the sweeping admiration of his glance. 'Quiet and beautiful, you are a woman of class, *chérie*. Or should I have said "neat, not gaudy"?'

She frowned at him and he clicked his tongue chidingly. 'It's a quotation from Charles Lamb, your namesake. I thought you were supposed to be an expert in English literature. You have a degree in it, do you not? And you live among books.'

'If one has it, one doesn't need to flaunt it,' she said primly. 'Have you been studying hard to impress me with your scholarship?'

'I like to read widely but studying is not my forte so I'm afraid I must decline the opportunity to flatter you with my devotion. I hope to impress you in other ways.' He accompanied his teasing purr with the polite offer of his elbow as they descended the wide staircase to the dining-room. 'I'm glad that you chose not to flaunt tonight, *chérie*. If you had worn your Mata Hari dress I would have had difficulty in treating you like the gently bred young lady you are.'

'Perhaps I don't want to be treated like a lady,' she flirted.

'In that case you must wait until after dinner,' he promised her in a satiny growl.

She discovered the reason for his unaccustomed restraint when they entered the dining-room. Already seated at the head of the long, narrow, highly polished table was an upright figure, shrunken with age inside his formal clothes.

Elizabeth was speechless as Jack introduced her with a stately flourish to Alain St Clair, whose beringed fingers seemed too heavy for his pale hand as he raised hers to his mouth and saluted her with a practised gallantry to match his grandson's.

The old man's eyes were a darker version of Jack's, slightly rheumy but acutely penetrating for all that, and Elizabeth briefly panicked at the notion that his X-ray vision might perceive his priceless necklace beneath the draping fabric of the cowl. The danger of it being discovered in her room by curious servants had outweighed the slight risk that Jack might seek to undress her before she could excuse herself for a few minutes.

She blushed at her thoughts and Alain St Clair smiled puckishly and murmured something in rapid French to his grandson that made him grin. Elizabeth forgot her small deception about not speaking their language, and bristled with outrage. Why, the sly old fox! Jack had led her to expect a tottering but dignified and elderly autocrat... not this wicked old reprobate.

'If I am an *ingénue* at my age, *monsieur*, it is not because I am *ingénieux*—ingenious—but because I have always *previously* associated with gentlemen,' she said crisply as she took the seat to his right that he had indicated and swept them both with a look of chilly disdain. 'And if I am ripe it's not for the plucking but for delivering the lesson in manners that you both richly deserve!'

As soon as the words were out she was appalled at her rudeness but Alain St Clair only laughed, a boisterous sound from such an apparently frail chest that mingled with Jack's smooth, 'Did I not mention, *Grandpère*, that Eliza-Beth speaks our language fluently? Possibly because she forgot to mention it to me. So *chérie*, I am pleased that you have understood everything that I have said to you in the throes of my most... *ungentlemanly* conduct.'

This, too, entertained the old man. As dinner was served Elizabeth noticed a spark of mild antagonism between the two men underlying their obvious affection and wondered whether they had had some prior argument and whether it had been about her. Her discomfort was eased when she realised that Jack appeared as suspicious as she of the sudden rally in his grandfather's health. His conversation was peppered with pointed offers to assist in the cutting up of meat, the picking up of the heavy solid silver condiments and pious cautions about the mixing of wine with prescription drugs until his grandfather snapped testily that he was not going to lie down in his grave just because Jack had decided he wanted his inheritance early. For some reason the reply seemed to satisfy Jack and he returned to his former path of subtly flirting with his eyes at Elizabeth across the hot-house roses which bloomed between them in a chased-silver bowl.

Although Alain St Clair proved to speak English as faultlessly as his grandson, in deference to his years they spoke French during the meal, and after Elizabeth had conquered her embarrassment and firmly thrust her guilt to the back of her mind she actually enjoyed herself. The old man knew more about rare books than anyone she had ever met, including her uncles, and his conversation was sharp—witty, arrogant and very opinionated in his beliefs, drawing her out into the kind of furious debate that revealed the fiery emotionalism she usually eschewed.

Elizabeth had no difficulty at all in imagining him and Uncle Miles and Uncle Seymour in a huddle over their port and brandy, three eccentric old men like witches around a brew, debating books and the sad decline of the world from the standards of their youth, heads filled with over two hundred years of combined life-experience coming to the certain conclusion that the modern generation were leading the world to rack and ruin by ignoring the shining wisdom of their elders and betters.

Dinner had begun at an elegantly late hour and it was after eleven when Alain St Clair rose, looking much less robust than he had earlier, and he didn't demur when Jack firmly suggested that he forgo his usual port and forbidden cigar before bed.

'No doubt I shall be seeing much of you now that you have finally found your way here,' he murmured obscurely to Elizabeth as he bent creakingly over her hand. He addressed himself to his grandson. 'Now, *mon petit-fils*, you will help me up to my room. I do not wish to disturb André this late and, besides, it is necessary for me to have a few words with you before you retire.'

With a silent gesture that she interpreted as a request for her to wait for his return, Jack assisted his

grandfather from the room and Elizabeth was left with
only her half-empty coffee-cup and the discreet whispers of the servants removing the debris of the meal.
After they had gone she sat in exquisite isolation and
listened to the measured tick of the ornate clock on the
marble mantelpiece above a fireplace that was surely
only ornamental in the sub-tropics.

She sat for so long that she began to imagine that the
shadows in the corners of the chandelier-lit room were
moving. She tapped her fingers uneasily on the arm of
the chair. She finished her wine and put the wine glass
down on the pristine table, rising restlessly to her feet
and pacing the room.

She had come to a decision. Thankfully tonight had
proved to her complete satisfaction that Alain St Clair
was not the sternly self-righteous ogre conjured up by
her guilt-ridden imagination. Her fear that he would
immediately demand the arrest and prosecution of her
uncles was groundless, as was the anxiety that his heart
might not be equal to so great a shock. Judging from
his cynicism at dinner, Alain St Clair was virtually un-
shockable, and he had revealed a mistrust of authority, born in the war, which extended to all
representatives of officialdom. If there was punishment or revenge to be administered he would, like
Jack, be far more likely to take care of it himself than
brook outside interference into his private affairs.

However, she didn't think that the Alain St Clair she
had met tonight would think in terms of punishment
when she handed back his property and questioned the
inexplicable mix-up in shipping which Uncle Seymour
had sadly taken temporary advantage of. With his
depth of human understanding, coupled with a devil-

ishly ironic sense of humour, Monsieur St Clair would probably find the whole sorry episode amusing once he knew that he had suffered no lasting loss.

And Jack? Her heart was foolishly optimistic.

He would be relieved, wouldn't he, that the 'deeper game' she had been playing had been nothing more than an honest desire to right a wrong? And no doubt order a complete inventory of the château's contents to make sure that no other careless breaches of security had occurred—if that was indeed what had happened.

That wouldn't be his *first* reaction, of course. She knew what *that* would be. She had already learned how volatile he could be under that ultra-disciplined façade. Coward that she was, she thought she would ask his grandfather to explain everything while she stayed discreetly out of the way, until the dust had settled sufficiently for him to listen to reason.

Suddenly the doors to the dining-room burst open, slamming back against the pale walls, and Jack strode in, in the grip of a magnificent fury.

'So! You beautiful, conniving bitch! You are a thief, nothing but a common thief!'

He grabbed her, slamming her bottom against the bevelled edge of the table as he arched her back until her expression of wide-eyed horror was starkly illuminated by the pool of light cast by the central stem of the chandelier.

'You do well to look terrified, *chérie*,' he snarled as his hands wrapped with loving violence around her throat, his eyes silver daggers that slashed her with razor-sharp contempt, 'because I am very close to giving in to my most primitive instincts! You played me well,

didn't you, you——?' He used a French obscenity that
made her blanch.

'To appear so inept at deception when you are really so incredibly skilful,' he sneered, 'so vulnerable
when you are as hardened as an old whore. And that
is all you are to me, *chérie*, a lying, cheating whore. In
spite of all my suspicions I actually had *faith* in your
non-existent integrity!' He laughed rawly, in savage
self-derision. 'How arrogant I was, when all you were
doing was using me for access to a bigger bounty—I
suppose you would have whored with my grandfather,
too, if he had proved himself as gullible as I!

'But you won't get away with it, you treacherous
bitch, so you may as well tell me what you have done
with it—tell me what you have done with *La Flèche de
St Clair*!'

CHAPTER TEN

'*LA FLÈCHE DE ST CLAIR*? The arrow? What arrow?'

Her strained whisper seemed to fan his white-hot rage. He applied an even greater pressure to her throat, forcing her flat against the table as he loomed over her.

'The necklace, Beth, as if you didn't know! And don't try that dewy-eyed look of bewilderment on me because it won't work any more. It's a lie—and *this* is the truth!'

'This' was a crashing blow against the table beside her head that vibrated her skull against the wood. The hand that encircled her throat closed on her jaw and wrenched her head roughly sideways so that she was forced to confront the cut-out pages of the shabby book as he fanned them furiously bare inches from her cringing nose.

'Where is it, Beth?' he demanded savagely.

'If you'll just let me up I'll tell you,' she choked, trying to marshal her shattered courage. 'I can explain everything——'

'I'm sure you can, you little liar!' He jerked her head back again and thrust his grim face close to hers, speaking swiftly and with a lethal softness. 'But there is no explanation that can excuse this—*violation*! If you knew about *La Flèche*, then you knew that you were stealing the one prize that my grandfather managed to hide from the Nazis when they tried to wipe the St Clairs from the face of the earth.

'That necklace was made for my family in the seventeenth century—*La Flèche* is our sole connection with the past...our hope for the future! It *means* something to this family. The only way you could fence so unique a necklace is to break it up and sell the pieces, but of course that probably wouldn't bother you! Or were you planning to ransom it back to the insurance company——?'

'Jack, please—I wasn't trying to steal anything——' She stopped as he shifted his hand back to her throat, choking off the words.

'Lying slut. I found this in your room, along with the rest of your cache!' From lightning-softness to cracking thunder! Elizabeth's burning ears rang with the ugly accusation. 'No wonder you jumped when I walked in on you in the library this morning! I must have nearly caught you in the act!' He slammed the table again, punctuating his furious self-contempt. 'I *knew* you were hiding something, I knew it! But, God forgive me for being a fool, I thought it was something *innocent*——' he spat out the word as if it revolted him '—like trying to charm *Grandpère* into selling you more of his books, or querying him about a suspect provenance of one he had sold you...'

'I haven't been trying to steal the necklace, Jack,' she croaked insistently. 'For God's sake—I've been trying to give it *back*!'

Deep, dark colour flushed across his face as his lips pulled back in a rictus of a smile. 'You take me for a fool?' he demanded fiercely, leaning into her so that she felt the hard grind of his hips against her trembling belly and the grate of her spine against the table.

'No—Jack—I'm telling the truth this time.'

'Huh!' The pressure didn't ease one iota. Elizabeth thought about bursting into tears but she realised he would probably enjoy hearing her sob—or, worse, think that she was still trying to manipulate him with her vulnerability. She was bleakly aware of the miserable fate of the Boy Who Cried Wolf.

'It's true,' she said huskily, trying to speak calmly through her severely restricted airway. 'The necklace and those books—they were sent to my uncles by mistake in the crate with their purchases from your grandfather. Obviously your grandfather couldn't have packed them so it must have been someone who didn't know books, who didn't check the inventory properly, or was careless. By the time they realised what had happened my uncles were worried that they'd be accused of stealing...'

'Why—if they were totally innocent of guilt?' he challenged harshly. 'If they had returned everything straight away *Grandpère* would have been *grateful* rather than suspicious of any wrong-doing.'

Elizabeth swallowed, sternly reminding herself of the clean breast that she had promised herself to display. Her voice quavered bravely. 'Well, actually Uncle Seymour *did* find the necklace and the books more or less straight away but—well, he's old and he loves beautiful old things... Since no one was shouting for their immediate return he—he just thought that it wouldn't hurt if he enjoyed them for a while...

'He never intended to withhold his finding indefinitely,' she added desperately. 'He just looked on it as *minding*... And when Uncle Miles realised—well, they *did* try to arrange a return through the proper channels. Uncle Miles phoned and wrote, but your grandfather never replied and we couldn't just send the necklace back in the post! So—so I offered to bring it back and try and explain and apologise——'

'And since you were already set for a spy mission on Ile des Faucons it was all *incredibly* convenient!' There was not a shred of belief in the sardonic interruption, but imperceptibly the grip on her throat eased.

'It was the other way around,' she said quickly, hoping that the worst of the explosion was over and that now he would start to think. 'I told you the truth last night—the Corvell thing was sprung on me at the last minute at the airport. I had no idea that the Hawkwoods and St Clairs were the same family... or whether the disappearance of the necklace had even been discovered. I had to know what the situation was before I blundered blindly into it. I'd promised Uncle Miles that I'd be very discreet. Don't you see, I *had* to get into the estate and meet your grandfather before I could say anything...' Heartened by the slight easing of his hand, she ventured tentatively, 'Could you—do you think you could please get off me now? You're hurting me.'

She had misread his softening. He didn't budge. If anything his body settled more deeply on to hers, stressing the weakness of her position and the power of his. His eyes, as cold and grey as dead ashes, contrasted with the flaming tension that smouldered in the bunched muscles of his body.

'And you think you haven't hurt *me* with your litany of lies?' he grated. 'Did you think that I was so far under your spell that I would believe any ridiculous fabrication you chose to feed me?'

Her description of events sounded absurdly unbelievable even to her own ears, and the fact that some of his condemnation was deserved undermined her feeble flutter of confidence. His reaction seemed to confirm her earlier decision not to confide in him until she had proof of her honest motives.

She realised wearily that she was paying the price for two crimes here—one of which was not even her own. In Jack's mind she and the treacherous Zenobia had temporarily merged into one. The other woman had always been beyond any dream of vengeance, but she, Elizabeth, was right here, literally within his grasp.

'Look, you can call Uncle Miles and ask,' she said, struggling against a fresh desire to weep. 'He'll tell you——'

'Of course he would *lie* for you, if he was an accomplice. Was it he who wormed the information of the existence of the necklace and where it was kept out of *Grandpère*...?'

'Don't be ridiculous, he's seventy-two!' she snapped with a trace of her natural resilience.

'Age is no barrier to deceit.'

'I know what Seymour did was wrong, but it wasn't his *intention* to deceive,' she cried. 'He's a very gentle and unworldly sort of man. What will you do? Please don't let my mistakes prejudice your actions. My uncles wanted so badly for things to be smoothed over that I don't think it occurred to them that I wouldn't succeed. They'd be horrified if they knew what had happened——'

'What you'd done, you mean?'

'Yes—no! I mean, yes, what I've *done*—not what you *think* I've done...'

'Bartering your body for a key to the kingdom of St Clair?'

'*No*! Don't you *dare* say it was that!' she said, reacting fiercely to his degrading reduction of what they had shared to its lowest physical denominator.

'Well, if you came all this way to return the necklace to its rightful owner, why didn't you mention the fact to my grandfather tonight?'

Because tonight had been forbidden magic. A little slice of heaven. She was accepted in his home—desired, admired, wanted...gracing his table and his bed in the bitter-sweet knowledge that she loved him and that this one last night might be all that she would ever have of him. She had selfishly wanted it to remain unblemished.

'I didn't know I was going to meet him,' she said defensively. 'I wasn't prepared... You said he was sick. I—I couldn't just blurt it out over dinner, so I decided to wait until tomorrow...'

'You mean until I was out of the way and you were free to play on his sympathy with your pathetic story?' He flayed her with the accuracy of his contemptuous guess.

'It was *his* property I was returning, not yours.' She flew the defiant tatters of her dignity at him. 'It was only right that *he* be the one to decide what to do!'

Her frustration at the hopelessness finally broke the bonds of her control. 'Oh, damn you, Jack, let me go. *Please*. I can't even *think* with you lying on top of me!'

Her outburst left her panting, having exhausted her temporary store of oxygen. He rode the rise and fall of her chest with crushing ease.

'I know the feeling, *chérie*.' For the first time she caught a glimmer of light in the cold slate eyes, but no mercy. He straightened at last, but there was no escaping the prison of his body. His thighs still trapped hers against the table-edge as she slowly pushed herself up off the dark mirrored-polish of its surface and his hands settled heavily on her aching shoulders. 'So where is the necklace now? I presume it's still hidden somewhere on the premises. I certainly didn't find it when I turned over your room.'

He had searched through her things. What hadn't occurred to her in the initial shock of his attack now made her recoil against an unexpected feeling of violation that must be a pale imitation of what he was feeling. 'What made you look there in the first place?' she asked shakily, mistrusting his sudden calm.

'Ironically enough I called in to leave a token of my grandfather's misguided esteem on your bed ... at his request,' he said drily. 'A rare edition of seventeenth-century poetry that he thought would be an appropriate gift for such an "impassioned intelligence" ...'

'So you decided to search my room while you were there,' she said bitterly. 'I thought you said you had faith in my integrity?'

'*Had*, yes.' He stressed the past tense bitterly, a fresh flame kindling in his smouldering gaze. 'Until I saw the interesting collection of bedside reading on your dressing-table. You were too cunning for your own good, *ma petite voleuse*. Were you working on the

Edgar Allan Poe theory that guilt is best hidden in plain sight?'

'They *weren't* in plain sight—I left them in my suitcase, not on the table!' She threw his own lie back in his face. When her bag had arrived she had wrapped her precious cargo in her most intimate underwear and thrust it into the back of the antique wardrobe.

He surveyed her with a grim smile of malice. 'If you intend to make a living as an upper-class cat-burglar, *chérie*, you'd do best to learn the aristocratic rules of etiquette. Guests dress—maids unpack. No doubt one of *Grandpère*'s efficient army freshened your room for the night ahead and was over-zealous in her helpfulness.'

Jack's hands tightened on her shoulders and he gave her a small, vicious shake. The calm had only been the eye of the storm. 'Now no more stalling, Beth. I've given you all the rope you need to tie yourself up in your lies. Where have you put the necklace? Somewhere utterly bizarre, I suppose, to match the rest of your tale. And, I warn you, don't even *think* of using it to negotiate terms. I don't make bargains with criminals!'

Although she had bleakly anticipated his violent rejection, and thought she had prepared herself for its impact, Elizabeth found that she hadn't. How could she? She had never known such a devastating pain, as if she had been emptied of everything but the shattering knowledge that she had hurt him and that he would never let her get close enough to do that again. If she told him that she loved him now he would laugh in her face, and she only had herself to blame. He wanted no part of such a faithless love. She felt empty, scraped raw by his contempt and the realisation that with his words he was systematically destroying any possibility of reconciliation between them.

'I'm wearing it!' she said dully.

His reaction was dramatic.

He went rigid, jerking back from her as if she had just told him that she was contaminated by some dread disease. His face wore a look of shocked fascination.

'You're *what*?'

'I'm wearing it,' she repeated uneasily, bewildered by her sudden release. 'It seemed the safest way to carry it around since I couldn't just leave it lying in my room. Naturally I used the safe at the hotel,' she added hurriedly, thinking it was shock at her cavalier treatment of his precious heirloom that had prompted his violent recoil. 'But when I—I thought I might be able to find a way into the estate I decided it was better to wear it than carry it around in a bag that could get stolen. Not many people would realise the true value of the books offhand, but jewellery is something everyone can appreciate the value of——'

'You've worn it before tonight?' he interrupted softly.

'Yes, a couple of times,' she said uneasily, pressing her hand to her collarbone. His eyes followed her gesture as he muttered what sounded like a profane French prayer beneath his breath.

'Actually I was wearing it on the plane when we met, too,' she announced defiantly. Whatever unknown crime she had committed now, she might as well confess it all.

His eyes, which had been wide and pale, suddenly narrowed with a strange, dark intensity.

'*Mon Dieu*, you really do like to live dangerously...'

'No one's ever seen me wearing it,' she said, instinctively defending herself against the threat of that silky murmur. 'I always wear something high-necked if I put it on...'

'But it's still there around your neck. Still being *worn*.' He lifted his head suddenly, his eyes catching the light, and she shivered at the predatory satisfaction that was starkly revealed there, as if he were a hawk brooding over a fresh kill.

'I want to see it,' he demanded.

Her fist clenched over her chest. 'You can't have it, not here. I'll have to unzip my dress to get it off——'

'I don't want you to take it off. I want to see you wearing it.'

He was laughing! A richly exultant sound of amusement that had the impact of a bomb in the quiet room, and before Elizabeth could react to his sudden, inexplicable change of mood he had grabbed her by the wrist and propelled her out into the hall.

'What are you doing? I told you I'd give it to you!' she panted as he dragged her up the stairs, leaving one of her shoes behind on the landing as he whirled her across it and up the next flight. By the time they reached the door to her room she was breathless with fear and excitement and wondering if one's body could drown in adrenalin.

'You don't have to do this, Jack——' she began but he unexpectedly ignored her room and plunged on down the dark corridor and round a corner.

'Oh, yes I do, *chérie. C'est le sort.*'

Fate? Elizabeth had thought that Jack was too much of a fighter to be a fatalist. Up a few more steps and around another corner and she found herself blind in the middle of a black room.

The light snapped on and she blinked awkwardly and saw Jack leaning back against the closed door, staring at her, still in the grip of what was obviously some fiercely exultant emotion.

'Show me,' he commanded, and stood, legs planted astride, hands hanging loosely at his sides, the picture of a relaxed man prepared to explode into violent motion at a moment's notice.

Automatically Elizabeth turned away from the powerful image of daunting male arrogance and her eyes took in what her mind had subconsciously registered even before the light had been switched on.

Not her bedroom. His. He had brought her to his room, his territory... his rules.

The heavy blue silk-damask curtains were drawn at the double windows, increasing the closed-in intimacy created by the pale blue and gold figured wallpaper and the ornately carved plaster ceiling. A huge bed was turned down invitingly to reveal fine, pure white embroidered linen beneath the deep blue silk comforter. A chair and a wardrobe like hers were the only other furnishings. A room as starkly masculine and as finely disciplined as its owner was... usually.

A drifting movement of air behind her warned Elizabeth too late, and before she could turn the fabric across her shoulders suddenly gave way as her zip was drawn down to her waist. She swung around, supporting her loose bodice protectively with her hands over her breasts, the wide, slanting shoulders of her dress dropping down her arms.

'Jack...' Her protest faded away when she saw him staring at the first gleam of gold revealed by the slipping gown. The earlier tension was still in him but it was tension now of a different sort. Moody possessiveness glittered in his eyes, along with a kind of savagely amused tenderness that was like a balm to her self-inflicted wounds. Her fluttering fear that he intended to take his revenge by forcing her in a physical expression of his contempt died. Jack would never force her—he would never have to. Whatever he wanted she would give him willingly, gratefully... needing the chance to atone at least partially for the sin of her betrayal...

He reached out and threaded his fingers gently under the sleeves of her dress, holding her wide, wondering and slightly wary eyes with his own hypnotic silver gaze as he tugged, slowly and inexorably dragging the sleeves further down her arms. 'I want to see,' he said, in a rough whisper that curled caressingly around her sense.

The zip was only partially unfastened and the dress caught in folds at her waist but he was too absorbed in his discovery to notice. He stared at the blaze of red and gold and diamond fire that hug from her neck, mantling her pale skin from collarbone to the upper reaches of her breasts where they swelled above their twin cups of pale green lace. His eyes narrowed and Elizabeth had the fleeting feeling that he was studying her with the detached eye of a connoisseur rather than that of a passionate lover.

She drew a ragged breath and her breasts quivered, setting the fiery jewels a-splinter with light.

'Oh, yes, they suit you well . . .'

He reached out and touched the central stone, an oval-cut red ruby suspended from a fan of overlapping chased-gold links. He pressed on it lightly until it sank into the whipped-cream cushion of flesh, and then he ran his finger up the chain that disappeared around her neck.

'Do you know why it's called *La Flèche*?' he murmured, moving closer as he studied the tiny overlapping triangles. 'Because these are tiny arrows, all pointing down . . .' He traced his finger back down again. 'Down towards a woman's secret heart... Many women have worn this necklace for the men of my family in the past three hundred years. It's in the nature of a ritual. And all the St Clair males have their duty to perform in this secret ritual . . .'

To Elizabeth's delicious consternation his finger continued on down past the necklace, over the rise of her left breast, skimming the lace that covered her trembling heart, down over the soft bunch of material at her waist to press lightly into the V between her legs.

'To pierce his woman's body with the arrow of possession, that is the St Clair male's task . . . And if she is proudly wearing the badge of that possession there is no escape from destiny . . .'

'I . . . I don't understand,' she murmured.

He smiled, his eyes slitting as he watched her sway helplessly to his feather-light caress. 'You will, *chérie* . . .'

'You're still angry.' Her aching uncertainty was in

every aching syllable and he made no attempt to assuage it.

'Yes. But that will add an element of uncertainty that will be rather stimulating for us both, will it not?' His finger curved inwards, stroked, and Elizabeth melted inside. He took his hand away and she felt empty, abandoned.

'No——'

He misunderstood, his eyes dominating hers as he forced her chin up and let her see the full force of his masculine intent in a face taut with barely leashed hunger.

'*Yes*. You have the instincts of a born gambler, Elizabeth, though you may try to deny it. You have a reckless streak in you that you explain away as stubbornness but which I recognise, for it is a trait we share. You gambled on coming to my island, you gambled when you spied on me and taunted me with your inconsistencies, and you gambled again when you welcomed me into your body with such voluptuous enthusiasm and then tried to primly pretend that it hadn't happened. And most of all, *ma chère*, you gambled on coming here and expecting me to let you walk away afterwards as if I didn't exist....'

He fingered the tiny satin bow that was the front fastening of her bra as he looked into her eyes. He held her breathless gaze as they both heard the tiny click that signalled that he had slipped the fastening.

'Now you take the most exciting gamble of all, *chérie*.' He brushed the lace aside, still without lowering his gaze, and cupped her breasts, massaging them softly. 'You gamble that I am more honest with you than you were with me.'

'Jack——'

'No. I don't want to talk.' He lowered his eyes and looked at what his hands had done. Her breasts were swollen beneath their garland of precious stones, their tracery of blue veins boldly outlined against their taut paleness, the nipples cresting the heavy globes dark and stiff.

'Grandfather was right...you are ripe. Ripe and ready for this...aren't you, *chérie*, even if you don't realise it yet...?'

He put his mouth where his hands had been and she cried out, struggling to free her arms from the sleeves that held them to her sides, and he drew back.

'Yes, we'll take it slow this time, *ma chère*...long and slow. This is a first time for you, and I know that you might be afraid...'

The savage edge had gone, only the tenderness remained, and Elizabeth was more bewildered than ever.

'I don't know what you mean...' she whispered, trying to capture the elusive quality of his words.

He answered her question literally, stripping off his jacket, and tie and shirt, and throwing them to the thick, richly patterned square of carpet beneath their feet. 'The first time in my bed.'

He reached around her and drew the zip fully down, his furry chest brushing her nipples, making her heavy breasts ache. He helped her step out of her dress, careful not to touch her with his hands, and threw it on top of his clothes. The bra was hanging open from its shoulder-straps and he slid it down her arms and on to the floor. He was naked before she, because he wouldn't let her take off her silky green pants or the heavy necklace.

He was aroused, and with each slow movement seemed to become more so until every muscle in his body corded with the effort of restraint. And still he didn't rush her.

Elizabeth was in a state of feverish wonder, hardly able to believe that the man who had threatened to kill her only a short while ago had suddenly become this mellow god of sweet gentleness, but content to accept the unexpected gift and worry about motives tomorrow.

The necklace sliding against her body particularly seemed to fascinate him. He turned and arched her in his arms so that he could admire the way it shifted and settled against her pale satin skin. When he placed her on his bed he took the time to arrange it to his artistic satisfaction before he bent and nuzzled her over, above and between the precious curves and curlicues, murmuring with fascination over the contrast between succulent, warm flesh and cool metal. He kissed her and stroked her hair from its neat rolls until it rained darkly across his white pillow. He ran his hands over her sides, tracing the billowing lines that he praised with erotic words of desire, his fingers teasing up the wide, silky legs of her pants until he became impatient with the barrier to his full enjoyment of her body and tore them in a hiss of splitting stitches. He cupped and suckled her breasts, so gentle that he caused her pain, his tongue drawing out the nipples until they glistened like the rubies that he so admired. He stroked her slightly rounded belly and kissed it, and murmured something secret into the pale, soft down that grazed its surface and then he parted her thighs and praised her there, too, in ways that made her writhe voluptuously in the crisp white sheets.

Elizabeth had naïvely thought she knew him as a lover. Now he showed her that she was wrong, that she didn't know him at all. He curbed and channelled her eagerness with a ruthless strength and a single-minded purpose that heightened her arousal until just the touch of his mouth brushing across her skin was an unbelievable delight, moving languidly on her, over her, in her, until she couldn't contain the building sensation any longer and exploded in an agony of pleasure, rising and falling feverishly beneath him until he grasped her by the hips and pinned her deep into the soft mattress in a powerful, bucking spasm that arched him like a bow and released him into soaring flight with a savage shout of victory.

Afterwards, as she lay tangled in his arms, still gasping for the breath that he had stolen out of her body, he raised himself up on one elbow and touched the necklace that she still wore.

'There's a family legend attached to the wearing of this . . . a very powerful legend that has come to be accepted as fact. Like this one, from the other side of my family . . .' he touched the ring in his ear ' . . . being considered a symbol of the reckless luck of the Hawkwood men in fulfilling their deepest aspirations.'

'Oh?' Elizabeth tensed at the silky satisfaction in the lazy drawl.

'Would you like to know what it is?' His silver eyes taunted her with their secrets. 'Ever since the necklace was made, as a betrothal gift for the bride of a pre-revolutionary St Clair, it has exhibited a peculiar power over the women who wear it——'

'It doesn't have any power over me. I don't even like it,' interrupted Elizabeth, quite truthfully.

'Ah, but you see, *chérie*, its power has only just been given its chance to begin to work on you...'

She was alert now to the danger-signals in his dark smile, and sat up, regarding him warily as he lay back against his high pillows.

'The flight of an arrow must terminate within its vessel—and you, *ma chère*, have just received a quiver-full...'

It took a moment for the penny to drop.

'You mean——'

'I mean that it is a potent fertility charm. Any woman who accepts her St Clair lover while wearing that necklace is destined to be pregnant with a male child within the year...'

Elizabeth bunched the sheets around her as she rose up on her haunches, vibrating with outrage that he could frighten her so. 'That's ridiculous—it's just an absurd story! Surely you don't believe that superstitious rubbish?'

'Absurd stories seem to be the norm tonight,' he replied smoothly. 'You may call it superstition, *chérie*, but in three hundred years the necklace has never failed, even on women who were thought to be barren. I did not protect you this time—there seemed no point, since your pregnancy was a predestined inevitability from the moment I entered you...'

She was wrestling frantically with the clasp to the necklace, at the same time trying to keep the sheet covering her breasts, only to fail in both and end up kneeling before him in a provocative pose of rosy nakedness that made him grin approvingly.

'Damn you, take this thing off!' She presented her stiff back to him and he saluted it with a series of slow kisses before he rose behind her, deliberately taking his time to untangle the delicate gold fastening from the strands of hair that had become caught there.

'It's too late, Eliza-Beth, the deed is done; you are already fertile with my seed—soon your womb will swell with my bounty. A baby, to suckle life from where I have suckled pleasure in the process of his creation,' he murmured, looking down over her shoulder to where her swaying breasts displayed the soft red marks of his lovemaking.

'You're just saying this to frighten me, to punish me because I damaged your stupid male pride!' Elizabeth accused him wildly as the necklace suddenly slid from her neck to pool on the tangled sheets and she leapt out of his bed, almost falling in her haste to be free of his cruel taunting.

'Would it be such a punishment to bear my child?'

'Yes. *Yes!*' She denied him the wild truth of her heart, hating him for the method and unbelievably ruthless calculation of his revenge. The fact that he had deliberately not used any contraception she could almost forgive, since she had abrogated that responsibility herself, but to gloat about the possibility of making her bear an unwanted, illegitimate child created from a moment of casual lust was utterly unconscionable!

'I hate you!' she cried viciously. 'And rather than bear any child of yours I'd, I'd——'

'You'd what?' His voice was no longer lazy or taunting, but hard and sharp as steel as he rose from the bed to confront her in the full threat of his possessive masculinity. 'Beth——'

That strange hoarse note in his voice was another trick. She wouldn't listen.

'You're sick, you know that? You don't *deserve* to have any children and certainly none of mine!' It was the greatest insult she could think of. She longed to fling at him that she'd rather have an abortion. But she couldn't. Not even in the depths of her greatest torment could she ever kill their child. It might be illegitimate but it wouldn't be unwanted, and would never be lonely or unloved. But she would be damned if she would give him the satisfaction of knowing that.

'It's just stupid superstition!' she said wildly. 'But if it *did* happen you'd never know! Because I'd hide at the ends of the earth rather than let you near your son! And I'd never tell him that he was the spawn of a devil without a soul!'

CHAPTER ELEVEN

'So THIS is what the end of the earth looks like?'

Sitting at the top of a slightly rickety ladder in the poetry section of the narrow shop, Elizabeth wobbled dangerously as she stared down into the dark, mocking face that she hadn't seen for almost a month. Twenty-eight horrible, infinitely elastic days that seemed to have the ability to stretch themselves out until it seemed they would never end.

'W-what are you doing here?' she said uncertainly, wondering if she was talking to just another fevered illusion, the cunning work of a weary mind that had only just conquered an anguished fixation that every black head in a crowd was a taunting Frenchman with a smile of ice and a heart as metallic as the flash of gold in his ear.

'Where else would a devil without a soul be except wandering the depths of purgatory?' So he remembered every bitter word of that last horrible night. Good! So did she. Unfortunately she also remembered that not all of it had been horrible. 'Actually I'm here on a mission from my grandfather.'

Elizabeth's hands clenched on the catalogues in her lap. She couldn't believe the old man would be that cruel. He *knew* the way she felt about his son. Knew that she hated Jack and that Jack despised her. She had told him. She had practically sobbed her life story out on his shoulder as she begged him to arrange for her to leave the Isle of Hawks, and he had been very kind, considering that she had forced her way past his outraged manservant at the crack of dawn and confronted him while he was still in bed. He had patted her on the hand and thanked her for returning his property at such enormous stress to herself, and calmly ordered André to arrange for a helicopter and a connecting flight from Tontouta to Auckland. Elizabeth, who had spent the rest of the hours of darkness lying stiffly awake on her bed waiting for a thundering assault on her door, and terrified by mental images of Jack stealing her babies, had been inexpressibly stricken when Alain St Clair had managed to spirit her away exactly as she had requested.

She had half expected to be stopped at the airport for some trumped-up charge which would hold her long enough for a deeply remorseful, or far more likely savagely angry Jack to snatch her back under his possessive control, but Alain St Clair's name had worked like magic, clearing her through Customs and Immigration and on to the plane before she could draw breath.

One consolation had been that at least she had finished the job that she had gone there to do. Her uncles would suffer no lasting damage from her reckless jaunt. About herself she wasn't so sure.

Now she looked inside herself for the courage to be civilised when she longed to fly down and tear him limb from limb. She had thought she loved him, but how could she love such a monster? How could she trust herself to make the right choices when he only had to touch her and she was overwhelmed with feelings and desires she couldn't control? The idea of being in helpless thrall to her sexual cravings for a man who despised her was more repulsive than the idea of herself as a closet nymphomaniac!

'I did write to your grandfather and explain that we wouldn't be doing any more business with him...'

'Yes, I know. He was very disappointed. He hoped I would be able to change your mind.'

'I never change my mind,' said she who had been so indecisive since she came back that she'd had a hard time even selecting what to have for dinner each night. She picked at a bit of fluff on her winter skirt. She had lost some weight in the last few weeks but her warm winter tights and thick sweater probably made her look even fatter. Her hair was falling out of a silly bun and she knew she looked awful. He, in contrast, looked wretchedly marvellous, lean and beautiful, even in the open trench coat that was spattered on the shoulders with rain.

'Won't you come down and talk to me, Eliza-Beth?'

She hadn't heard her name drawled that particular way for a lifetime. Tears filled her eyes. She had been very emotional lately and she knew her uncles were worried. They tiptoed around her as if she was an invalid, or dangerously insane. And maybe she was. She wanted nothing more than to fling herself off the ladder into his arms.

But, 'No!' she retorted.

'That's a pity.'

'Why?'

'Because I wanted to talk to you about something.'

Elizabeth discovered that she had snapped the ballpoint pen she had been holding and she frowned as she scrubbed busily at the blue marks on her palm.

'Eliza-Beth?' The voice was warm and soft, like the air on his sub-tropical island, which wasn't fair because she knew he was neither.

'What?' she snapped, glaring down at him. She liked being this far above him, mentally as well as physically. It felt right.

He looked up at her, hands on his hips tucking the coat back to reveal black jeans and a cream sweater. He raised his voice over the brief roar of traffic as another customer entered the shop. 'Have you had your period yet?'

Elizabeth jerked in horror as several browsing heads lifted, and the ladder wobbled again, violently this time. She screamed and grabbed at the sides, showers of catalogues sliding off her lap and raining down on Jack's head as the whole precarious structure teetered and fell, tumbling her precisely where she had wished to be for the last several weeks.

'*Chérie ...*' She trembled at the familiar feel of his body against her, heat flooding into her cold heart. 'For God's sake, you shouldn't be up ladders with your risk of vertigo——'

The warmth washed into her pale face as she pulled away from him, smoothing down her clothes with shaking hands. 'It wasn't vertigo, it was *you*. How dare you come into my shop and ask me something like that!'

'I didn't think you'd agree to see me anywhere else,' he said with a meekness that she didn't trust, tucking one wayward strand of her hair behind her small ear.

'Don't——'

'Touch you? I can't help it. I've been thinking about it for weeks.'

'Well, I'm not pregnant, so you can stop thinking about it.'

He looked at her bulky sweater where it bunched over the waistband of her woollen skirt. 'Are you sure?'

'Of course I'm sure,' she hissed viciously, impulsively hauling up the bottom of her sweater to show him her slightly trimmed waistline. 'See!'

'You probably wouldn't show yet anyway,' he said, gently tucking the sweater down, his grey eyes as clear as the rain outside the window.

'I tell you, I'm not pregnant!' she insisted, blushing as she caught the eye of a customer hovering around the counter behind him. Jack glanced over his shoulder and one brutal look sent the man scuttling for the door. 'Now look what you've done. He might have been going to buy something!'

'Stop trying to change the subject, Beth——'

'I've *told* you, I'm not pregnant. How many times do I have to say it before you believe me?'

'I don't think I ever will.'

She gaped at him.

His grey eyes were steady, his hand not quite, as he smoothed it over his damp head in the first gesture of nervousness she had seen him make. 'So I suppose the only way I can be sure is to hang around...'

'For how long?' Elizabeth sneered to cover the searing delight that flared through her veins. 'Until next month? Until the end of the year when that stupid myth is finally revealed for the superstition it is?'

'Oh, I couldn't let that happen,' he said, his eyes darkening. 'I couldn't let the legend of the St Clairs be proved a fraud. I shouldn't have mocked you with it, but, as you know, I was angry for what I saw as your lack of faith——'

'*My* lack of faith?' she interrupted.

'—and it got out of hand. I didn't mean to hurt you, only teach you a lesson. As it was I was the one who learnt a painful truth. As *Grandpère* pointed out when I turned my surly temper on him, it was a matter of personal priorities and I had failed to accept yours as being as important to you as mine are to me. You make me drunk with a sense of my own power, *chérie*. My emotions tend to get out of hand around you—you make me vulnerable as I have not been in five years, and I don't always like it. I react badly sometimes. I joke. I am cynical. I experience inappropriately aggressive male behaviour.'

His eyes gleamed with a spark of humour at her astounded reaction to his humble litany, making her realise how bleak and lifeless they had been before. 'We strike sparks, we two, and because of that rare quality between us we bite and scratch when we know that in reality we want to love and kiss,' he went on. 'I liked provoking you only because I knew what sweet reconciliations would follow. So to demonstrate my good faith I have brought it with me...'

'Brought what?' Elizabeth asked.

He put his hand in his pocket and withdrew a handful of glitter.

'You've been walking around with it in your *pocket*?' she spat incredulously, trying to push the necklace back. 'You could have been mugged!' The thought of him lying bleeding in some dark alley made her blanch. 'Haven't you got any sense? I thought you were supposed to be security-conscious——'

'Without you I have no reason for security. Here. It's for you.' He turned over her hand and placed it across her palm, folding his on top. 'Next time you wear it for me I'll know that you have forgiven me.'

'Next time?' she said faintly, feeling the heat of his hand go all the way up her arm to explode in the pulse at her throat.

'Oh, there will always be a next time for us, *chérie*, if you want there to be...' he said softly. 'You were too *uncertain* and I was *too* certain. I demanded your trust before you were free to give it. I was sure I wanted to spend my life, have my children with you, and like a child myself I decided to take what I wanted. I was greedy. This time we will take it slow.'

'Slow?' Elizabeth stared at the object between their hands, realising what it had taken for a proud man to come to her and admit his faults. She too had let her pride come between them, and that stupid lack of self-confidence that had assured her that such a man could not possibly want her for herself alone... She looked at him, at the thin, controlled line of his mouth and the narrowed silver eyes which masked his inner thoughts and she smiled suddenly, ruefully, as she realised that she didn't have to try and read him; she could guess what was going on inside that handsome head. She knew him better than she had thought.

This, too, was a gamble for him, and one in which he clearly thought he had stacked the odds. If he had come this far, it was not on the off-chance of success. For all his appearance of humbleness he was enjoying the delicate battle, silently anticipating victory. For Jack Hawkwood was never one to underestimate his opponent. He had calmed down. He had thought. He had weighed and assessed the nuances of her behaviour. He had known, thank God, since he had walked through the door of the shop and seen her haunted violet eyes explode with pain and joy.

'How slow is slow?'

A lambent flame licked across the silver eyes. 'As slow as you like, *chérie*,' he said with a purring promise that made her breathless.

'Liar.'

'I love you and I have brought you my betrothal gift. If you love me you will wear it ...'

'And?' Her eyes were vivid with promise.

'And marry me.' The shining violet eyes dimmed the tiniest fraction and he continued smoothly, 'And make mad, passionate love to me all night in my hotel room until I have made you pregnant and your uncles force me with their shotgun to marry you, and my family honour is not tainted by rumours that the necklace has lost its devastating efficaciousness.' He watched with amusement the smug look of satisfaction that curved her small, kissable mouth. His Beth was definitely going to be a challenge.

'If I'm not home tonight my uncles will worry,' she said, peeping at him through her lashes.

'Just a quick one, then,' he agreed blandly.

'*Jack*!' He laughed and swung her round and she allowed him to kiss her, letting thousands of dollars drip carelessly through her fingers until he caught them and thrust them back into his pocket.

'I love you more than all the diamonds in the world,' she confided needlessly, when she resurfaced, prompting another submersion in the pleasure of a loving embrace.

'My uncles . . .' she murmured finally, as she tried to remember that she was a respectable businesswoman and shouldn't be kissing on company time. She had already heard one irascible old customer stomp past with a mutter about 'promiscuous, long-haired louts'!

'I have seen them already, I confess,' he whispered into the tiny, sweet-tasting hollow behind her ear. 'They are not averse to the novel idea of living in a château, especially one crammed with books, and perhaps you might care to run your business from there— *Grandpère* has many international connections that could be valuable to you. There is plenty of room, *chérie*, for I don't intend for you to fill *all* the rooms with children . . .'

'But the sooner we start the sooner we'll be finished,' she teased him, eyes dancing, and as he bent to kiss her again a vagrant thought floated up through her consciousness.

'Jack . . . you don't think that it's odd that Uncle Miles and Uncle Seymour never mentioned how well they got on with your grandfather? They let me think he might be an ogre!'

'Hmm?' His mouth wandered down the line of her jaw.

'Or that your grandfather never said why he didn't answer all those calls and letters, even though he must have realised they were important . . .'

'Hmm . . .'

'Or that he didn't turn a hair when I finally told him about the necklace...or seem to worry about how such an awful mistake could happen in the first place...' He nipped her throat and she gasped. 'And don't you think it's funny that your grandfather should have said that about me having "finally found my way" there when he didn't even know that I was coming——?'

'Beth?'

'Yes?' Her eyes widened at his impatient growl.

'No more detective work, please; the last case you handled was a disaster! The conspiracy theory might have some merit but, personally, *chérie*, I'd prefer to believe in the enchanting whims of fate and the beautifully wayward arrows of love. Not all the matchmaking relatives in the world would have persuaded me to marry the wrong woman...'

'Whereas I am very pleased to be marrying the wrong man!' stated Elizabeth firmly, and proceeded to prove it.

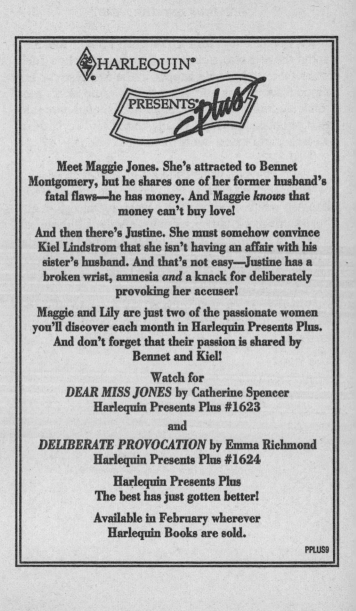

HARLEQUIN®

PRESENTS Plus

Meet Maggie Jones. She's attracted to Bennet Montgomery, but he shares one of her former husband's fatal flaws—he has money. And Maggie *knows* that money can't buy love!

And then there's Justine. She must somehow convince Kiel Lindstrom that she isn't having an affair with his sister's husband. And that's not easy—Justine has a broken wrist, amnesia *and* a knack for deliberately provoking her accuser!

Maggie and Lily are just two of the passionate women you'll discover each month in Harlequin Presents Plus. And don't forget that their passion is shared by Bennet and Kiel!

Watch for
DEAR MISS JONES by Catherine Spencer
Harlequin Presents Plus #1623

and

DELIBERATE PROVOCATION by Emma Richmond
Harlequin Presents Plus #1624

Harlequin Presents Plus
The best has just gotten better!

Available in February wherever
Harlequin Books are sold.

PPLUS9

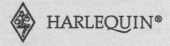

HARLEQUIN®

Don't miss these Harlequin favorites by some of our most distinguished authors!
And now, you can receive a discount by ordering two or more titles!

Share the adventure—and the romance—of

HARLEQUIN ◆ PRESENTS®

A Year
DOWN UNDER

If you missed any titles in this miniseries,
here's your chance to order them:

Harlequin Presents®—A Year Down Under

#11519	HEART OF THE OUTBACK by Emma Darcy	$2.89	☐
#11527	NO GENTLE SEDUCTION by Helen Bianchin	$2.89	☐
#11537	THE GOLDEN MASK by Robyn Donald	$2.89	☐
#11546	A DANGEROUS LOVER by Lindsay Armstrong	$2.89	☐
#11554	SECRET ADMIRER by Susan Napier	$2.89	☐
#11562	OUTBACK MAN by Miranda Lee	$2.99	☐
#11570	NO RISKS, NO PRIZES by Emma Darcy	$2.99	☐
#11577	THE STONE PRINCESS by Robyn Donald	$2.99	☐
#11586	AND THEN CAME MORNING by Daphne Clair	$2.99	☐
#11595	WINTER OF DREAMS by Susan Napier	$2.99	☐
#11601	RELUCTANT CAPTIVE by Helen Bianchin	$2.99	☐
#11611	SUCH DARK MAGIC by Robyn Donald	$2.99	☐

(limited quantities available on certain titles)

TOTAL AMOUNT	$
POSTAGE & HANDLING	$
($1.00 for one book, 50¢ for each additional)	
APPLICABLE TAXES*	$ _____
TOTAL PAYABLE	$ _____
(check or money order—please do not send cash)	

To order, complete this form and send it, along with a check or money order for the
total above, payable to Harlequin Books, to: *In the U.S.*: 3010 Walden Avenue,
P.O. Box 9047, Buffalo, NY 14269-9047; *In Canada*: P.O. Box 613, Fort Erie, Ontario,
L2A 5X3.

Name: _____

Address: _____ City: _____

State/Prov.: _____ Zip/Postal Code: _____

*New York residents remit applicable sales taxes.
 Canadian residents remit applicable GST and provincial taxes.   YDUF